I0693832

Novels from Odom's Library

The Ancient Ones

Connectivity

Papillon IV

Shorts from Odom's Library

The Last Trucker

Other short c.b.strul works currently in print

Spinners

Forget the Complex

What Grows from the Stump of a Tree?

PAPILLON IV

c.b.strul

Odom's Library

TABLE OF CONTENTS

May all beings
Including me
Be happy
Be healthy
Be free

PROLOGUE

THE WAY TO ODOM

Earth - Better Days

Ao had been fighting with her youngest sibling, Sid, over basically everything for the better part of two celestial turns and the other members of her community were getting fed up with the constant bickering between the children. Nikke was meant to be a place of peaceful enlightenment and common ground… hardly a place for arguing youths.

One day, Ao and Sid's fighting went too far. Sid accidentally let the cattle birds out of their pen and three of them actually managed to take flight on their tiny, pudgy wings. That was three fewer cattle birds from which the community of Nikke could harvest eggs for meal times, which was an obvious problem. And, even though Sid had been the one that let the cattle birds get away, Ao was the one who got called to the commissary to meet with the elder named Greck.

"Ao, my child," Greck spoke to the youth with weary in his voice, "it has come to my attention that you and Sid are not getting along. It is not good for youths to carry on in this way. Not good for the community."

"I'm sorry, elder," pled Ao. She did not wish to be in trouble. "But it wasn't me that lost those cattle birds. I swear it. Sid was the one who dropped the post. I was only trying to talk about something, and Sid let them run away."

"And why do you believe Sid did this?" Greck always had a way of making Ao feel uncertain of herself. It was as though the elder knew things about her that she couldn't hope to understand.

"I guess," Ao tried to see the other side – Sid's side, "I guess Sid was upset."

"Upset?" Greck leaned in, curiosity prickling up from his every pore. "Why should Sid have been upset, Ao?"

Ao had to think about that. Sid had been such a little pest lately. What was it about? "I guess, because I called Sid a little, goose bellied, horn eyed runt."

Greck sat back in his commissary seat, breathed out a huff of frustration, and, taking a huge chunk of cattle bird egg fluff in his hand, stuffed the pile of food into his mouth. *Ugh,* thought Ao, *he's gonna make me wait to receive my judgement.* She was really starting to hate it here in Nikke. Life was so boring. There was nothing for a girl her age to do for fun here. She watched Greck chew his egg fluff. His eyes never left her as he ate and that made her even more uncomfortable.

Finally, the elder swallowed the last of his pile and, to Ao's surprise, he smiled at her. "Ao," said Greck, "Nikke is hardly a place for a girl your age." *Had he read her mind??* "Usually, we would wait another season for this, but I think it's time you went to see Odom."

"Odom?" Ao had heard the name many times before. The elders had always said it with a strange sort of reverence. But, they had never told her who or what Odom was. A new, sinking feeling came upon Ao then, like she was about to be sent to prison for some crime of which she had wrongly been convicted. She argued, "I swear I'll be good elder, please don't send me to Odom." She started to cry.

Greck started to laugh. *What a jerk!* "So now you wish to stay? No. You don't know what you want out of life yet, Ao. You don't understand. I will not change my judgement. I will make a formal announcement to the community at the dinner tables tonight. And you will take the path along the north road tomorrow morning."

"But Greck, please!" Ao tried to plead once more.

Greck clearly did not appreciate this child using his private name in such a way. His eyes shone a fire within them. But, he contained himself. In a very calm voice he said, "You have much to learn, young Ao. Odom will make a fine teacher should he accept you into his library."

Ao was absolutely crushed as she left the commissary. Sentenced to leave Nikke, her community, her siblings. What would become of her in Odom's library? What if he didn't accept her in? What then? Would she be left to wander the back country alone for the rest of her life? She was too young, she thought, to be an exile. And what if Odom did accept her in? What then? Would she be a prisoner? A captive living a dreadful life doing… whatever it was folks were made to do in libraries? Then it occurred to Ao that she had never been to a library before. What even was a library? Cruelly, her mind went to the worst fantasies of hot mining facilities and cold gulags. She was a wreck – a sad, five-year-old, morbid wreck. Poor, poor Ao.

Next morning, Greck led Ao to the foot of the north road. Once there, he showed her the worn ivy path that trailed off through the chaparral and disappeared into the horizon. "How far will I have to walk?" Ao asked, nerves biting into her skull.

"Not long, Ao. This is not a death sentence, you know." Greck was trying to be nice to the girl, but she didn't know how to believe him. "Odom is a fine teacher. He even taught me when I was your age."

Ao was confused by this. She had to ask, "Odom's that old?"

Greck chuckled. "Technically, Odom is one without age. But, between you and me, yes. He is that old, and even older. Odom does not see the world as you or I. He is not constrained by time."

What was that supposed to mean, Ao wondered. How can anyone be without age or time? Now she really didn't want to leave. What in the world had Sid gotten her into?

"Follow this path," Greck pointed into the chaparral, "for thirty thousand steps. Harm will not come to take you should you keep your feet to the ivy. Once the sun has found its mount in the noon place of our sky, you should see the residence of Odom farther north. Walk straight to that structure. It is very large, but from the trail, you will find a canyon bridge that will lead you to a doorway meant for creatures of our size. That is Odom's guest entrance." But Greck saw the fear on young Ao. He knelt down to her level and took her hands in his own. "He is really quite friendly, Ao. Not a thing to be feared. Oh, yes," Greck remembered then the knapsack he had been holding for the girl, "I made you a noon meal so you will not be hungry on the path." Carefully, he strung the knapsack around the girl's shoulders – she did not outwardly show any new confidence, but Greck knew the knapsack would at least comfort her a little. "Now, off with you. May all your days be bright until our paths should cross again."

Ao walked the first ten thousand steps along the ivy path. At least, she thought it was ten thousand. She had lost count at around the one hundred mark. Regardless, the girl was hungry. So, she sat on a stone and pulled Greck's knapsack from around her shoulders. Inside, she found a container filled with a pile of egg. She hadn't expected anything different for she had never had a meal that wasn't egg in all her life.

Ao ate the whole pile in one go. *That was dumb,* she thought. *If I get hungry in the next ten thousand steps I'll have to remain hungry until I get there… that's a whole other ten thousand steps.* Ao shook her head. She was distraught and would have been absolutely inconsolable if anyone had cared to try and console her. She knew that much for certain.

However, the sun was peaking up from the clouds against the right hand corner of the sky and Ao realized that she didn't want to be late to the library even if it was a very scary place for her to have to go. If she were late, maybe she wouldn't be allowed in at all… and then she would definitely starve out here in the chaparral. Ao really didn't want to die alone in the wilderness, so she got up with Greck's empty knapsack and kept on walking.

Slowly, the ivy began to fade from the path. Slowly, the horizon cleared. And Ao could see the weird collection of tiny boxes that made up Odom's library in the vibrance of the noon light. That was her goal. But she was still so far away and her legs were getting tired and she was hungry again… because she had assured herself she would be by this time. Still, she kept walking. What else could she do?

Ten thousand more steps – she had tried harder to keep track this time – and Ao was crossing the canyon bridge. Not so scary actually. However, those tiny boxes had turned out to be much much larger than she had realized when she first saw them at noontime. *Buildings made for giants,* she told herself as she came closer. The thought had thrown off her count then, but she regained it with enough certainty to carry on.

When she got to the wall, there really was a door there. Greck had not been lying to her which was good. But, the door looked old, rusted, and uncared for, which was bad. Ao was so focused on the rusted metal that she missed seeing the piles of fresh flowers that lay out against the perimeters of those walls. She grabbed the creaky handle, opened the old door, and went inside – grateful and terrified that it had even opened for her in the first place.

Ao walked into a drippy, old hallway. "Hello?" She asked the room, "Is anybody here? Did I take too long on my walk? I swear I tried to keep count, but it was really hard."

No one was responding, so Ao cleared her throat once for good measure and continued her long walk through the hallway. She was careful not to step in the still puddles that lined the walls, but the one at the very end – where the room opened up into something like a cavern – was way too big and she would have to let her feet get a little wet if she wanted to keep going.

"Now my socks are soggy," the girl complained as she shuffled on through the alien space.

She stepped out of the water onto a weird, rubbery surface – porous – almost spongy – but surprisingly firm beneath her… It was a road of some sort. Down the way, there was even an old, dead vehicle lingering in the faded light of the open hallway door. Ao walked in that direction and the closer she came to the device, the more rust she saw there. *This is a prison,* she told herself. Ao really didn't like rust – it creeped her out. "Sorry, I really should be going," she said to no one. Then she turned around and began to run back toward the wet hallway, her soggy feet sending a squishy echo far down the chamber.

And then, there was a new light. It was coming toward Ao in a smooth, unimpeded line – floating through the darkness. The girl wondered if she might be seeing her first ghost. With that thought, Ao tripped and banged her knees against the road. "Ow," she shouted. It didn't actually hurt that bad, but it was quite a shock and she felt like the wind had been knocked out of her.

"Are you in trouble?" A mechanical voice spoke out from the place where the light had been only a moment ago.

Impulsively, Ao huddled herself up into a ball and whimpered, "Please don't hurt me."

"I would never," replied the voice. "You come from Nikke, I must presume. Did Greck send you, young one?"

Ao had already resolved herself not to speak with the voice, but its knowledge of those names sparked her curiosity. "How do you know Greck?"

"I am Odom," said the mechanical voice, "I taught him many turns ago when he was not much bigger than yourself. Are you here to learn as well?"

"I..." Ao's thoughts slipped away from her. She couldn't remember why she was here. She tried to focus. "I think I'm being punished."

"Oh?" Odom's voice was neither hostile nor judgmental — merely curious. "Thank you for being honest with me. You have nothing to fear of punishment so long as you reside within these walls, do you understand?"

Ao shook her head awkwardly as she attempted to peer through the darkness to see the face of the creature she was speaking to. But there was nothing there.

"Do you have a name?" Asked Odom, "For I have already told you mine."

"I'm Ao," said the girl.

"Can you stand, Ao? Or do you require assistance?"

The girl patted at her legs to be sure. She stood up saying, "I'm okay."

"Good. Let us walk." A floating orb illuminated in the dark place from where the voice had been sounding. Vibrant and hypnotic, it hovered through the air leading them slowly through the old, cavernous roadway. After a period of silence, Odom asked, "Why do you believe you are being punished, Ao?"

Ao tried to remember what she had told Greck back at the commissary, but the words wouldn't come. So, instead, she said what she knew was the simple truth. "I was mean to my youngest sibling, Sid. It was my fault that the cattle birds got out of their pen even though Sid's the one that dropped the post. I'm a mean jerk."

"I see," the voice from the orb replied. Ao didn't know why, but to her it seemed that the orb was laughing in that moment. *That's impossible,* she thought, *orbs of light can't laugh.* Of course, she had never seen an orb of light so much as speak before, but try telling a five-year-old that they don't already know everything and see where it gets you.

The cavernous roadway had many doors and the orb led Ao to one that still had a thin, false light lining it on all sides like a beacon. In Nikke, when the sun disappeared behind the horizon, most of the community would rally around campfires, so electrical, false light was a foreign concept to Ao who had not yet in her life ever needed such a thing. She felt in over her head as the door began to hum and open as if of its own volition. As the girl peered through, she saw a great, bright, new hall filled to the brim with technology. "What is this place," she asked, walking behind the orb through the stacks of active computing devices.

The orb disappeared then. But the voice of Odom remained. "This is my library. It is a part of me and the place from which I can share my knowledge most effectively with those who would learn. That is why you are here, is it not? To learn your lessons."

So a library is a place of learning, Ao told herself. To Odom she said, "I guess so?" It was more of a question really, but Ao was just so relieved to know that she wouldn't have to do a bunch of hard labor in some prison camp... not that there were any such places in the world anymore, but the children had always liked to tell each other scary stories about prisons after the sun went down and the campfires were lit. "Is it like story time?" She asked, not knowing where in this huge room to direct her voice.

"Yes," said Odom, his odd laugh returning once again. "It is a good deal like story time. Only, my stories will surround you. I will show you life as it was before. You will see and know how it truly was and, in the end, you will understand why Greck felt you had to come here." From one of the walls, a computer drive sprang open and an old hard drive floated down from a cubby until it reached a monitor device very near to the place where Ao stood. "Our first lesson," Odom told the girl, "is Papillon IV. Shall we begin?"

"Okay," Ao responded. What else was she supposed to say? And, from the monitor, a projection spanned out across the large room transforming everything around the girl. Ao stood suddenly in the middle of a distant memory – the ancient past.

BOOK I

PAULINE DELGADO

Earth - The Anthropocene Period

CHAPTER 1 - A TURNING POINT

The celestial year was Thirty Billion Five Hundred Million Sixty Three Thousand Four Hundred and Fifty Two… Three nodes from this very day. At this time in its history, the third planet in the Sol system of the Milky Way galaxy was headed down a bad path. The beings of Earth had long since forgotten how to care for their world, leaving fields of waste as far as the eye could see. Oceans, rivers, and lakes were overrun by the filth of humanity's neglectful behavior and the creatures who lived within those waters had become suffocated by the compounds of plastics, rot, and nuclear waste. A terrible stench perpetually filled the air which led the humans, distracted by their various devices, to wear odor relieving masks whenever they stepped outside.

On one particular day in that year, a youth by the name of Pauline Delgado walked to school with her two closest friends Zachariah and Estabon. Pauline was a bright girl in her age group – deemed high school juniors – often building up strange word groupings called poems on an app that helped her to find ever more elaborate ways to say simple phrases.

Once, she had managed to make the word marriage into a thirteen paragraph interpretation of the patriarchy's power over the women of her culture. Pauline had always been rather proud of that poem.

As she and her friends walked to school tinkering on their separate tablets and phones, they hardly even noticed the mounds of garbage that lined their path on all sides. They were numb to the situation as their society had trained them to be.

AO: It's so nasty there.
ODOM: Yes, it was a difficult time to be alive on this
    world, as it was on most.

Pauline Delgado's story begins within an overcrowded History classroom at the government funded Canard Public High School. Students were packed forty deep into such places and I believe the sheer number of humans in attendance across all of those classrooms could have been deemed a fire hazard if an independent assessor were ever allowed to survey one of those schools. Of course, this was never done as it would go against the various presidents' missions statements across the myriad regimes that had gained power in the nation of Brazil Superior during that period. Essentially, the overwhelming masses of trash mirrored that of the gross population levels all across the Earth. Brazil Superior is just one example. But, it is the most important one for our purposes at this time.

A woman named Mrs. Denise Rajado was Pauline's History teacher on that day. She was a hopeful woman, but very tired. She attributed her lack of energy to the government funding restraints, the limited pay, and the ever growing class numbers being placed before her. She never would learn about the cancerous mass that had formed against her brain stem several turns prior.

"Good morning class!" Mrs. Rajado shouted over the chattering students. The children did not seem to notice and continued talking or texting on their devices. "Children," the teacher shouted again, already in danger of losing the power within her vocal cords, "Please be silent!" Most of the class quieted down after that. "Now, we have a lot to cover today and not nearly enough time to get through it all," Mrs. Rajado began, "so if you will please bare with me."

Clicking on a tiny remote, Mrs. Rajado activated a primitive projector display which lit up the front wall as the room's other lights faded. What shone in that projection was the image of a massive ark spacecraft floating along on its journey between worlds.

"Who can tell me what this is?" asked the teacher.

Silence met the question at first.

A child coughed in the far back of the room.

Then, finally one of the students – young Zachariah – raised his hand and asked, "Is that a Papillon?"

"Yes, Zachariah," Mrs. Rajado replied with relief that one of her students had cared enough to respond, "this is Papillon I. About eight years ago, our government launched the first ark spacecraft in order to populate the recently terraformed world we call Adonis."

Mrs. Rajado clicked her remote again and the slide show continued presenting images of the ark spacecraft's launch, life onboard the ship along the journey, and Papillon I's eventual landing on the new planet.

"Obviously," continued the teacher, "the mission was a success or we probably would not be discussing it today."

Pauline became curious then and she raised her hand to ask, "Mrs. Rajado, what about the other Papillons? Why doesn't our syllabus talk about them?"

"Well, Pauline," Mrs. Rajado had always liked this particular student's strong will and attempts at discourse, "I don't think we'll see another Papillon launch for a while. You see, Papillon II disappeared before it reached its designated world and…"

There was a peculiar rumble in the room.

Mrs. Rajado decided to nip this in the bud, "Please turn off your phones during the lesson—"

But the rumbling was not simply a child's phone disrupting the class. It got bigger and louder until the ceiling tiles began to fall from their slats. Children were hit by heavier roofing and at least two of the students were knocked instantly unconscious.

Estabon yelled, "Earthquake!"

"Quickly!" Mrs. Rajado tried to act as she had been trained to do in such moments, "Under your desks!"

Some of the students heard her cry for reason and clambered down to their forearms to crawl beneath the tiny surfaces they used for study. Others, however, rushed to the classroom door, not willing to heed their teacher's advice.

"No! Come back here!" Cried Mrs. Rajado.

Pauline had been one of the students willing to listen to the adult in the room. But, as she lingered beneath her desk, a terrible odor crept into her nostrils. She asked so all the room could hear, "What's that smell?"

Too late, Mrs. Rajado realized the danger that staying in one place could present. She rose and began to say, "Hurry! We must run!"

The outside wall caved in then and a massive heap of sewage and trash burst into the room covering everyone within in gross, putrid waste.

A silence lingered for a long time. The remaining class had all been completely buried beneath the terrible mass. Some had already suffocated. Others had been crushed and would never again find strength within their limbs.

But, one hand did break free from the rubble. Pauline pulled herself up, nearly choking on the fumes as she went. The girl turned back and reached down for another's hand – Zachariah's. She pulled him from the mass, gagging and coughing, but alive. "Quickly," said Pauline, "we must save as many as we can!"

The students snapped into action, digging through piles of old pizzas and broken keyboards and blasting wrappings for sodas that would not break down for at least a thousand years. Pauline and Zachariah found one limp body here, another there beneath the garbage. Some of their classmates did survive the event. Others, unfortunately, did not. After much searching, Pauline snagged at her friend Estabon's hand from within the wreckage. But it was too late. The boy was not breathing and try as Pauline might, she could not get him to start again.

AO: Estabon died?
ODOM: He did, I am sad to say. And Mrs. Rajado as well.

All told, some thirty-eight intelligent beings lost their lives on that day. It was a terrible tragedy. However, from that moment came a turning point in the human species' collective acceptance of the reprehensible state of their planet. After all, when we learn to take responsibility for our actions, that is where progress begins.

In the evening of that very same day, Pauline stood before a small crowd of onlooking parents, children, and local media members. The setting was to be an all too quickly designated memorial park. That place, like all others on Earth, bore the same shameful loads of trash that had caved in from the side of the school. Truly, one could not find a pocket of real estate in all that land that did not wear the mark of thoughtless hoarding and reckless disposal.

As Pauline approached the podium, she tried to make a statement by pealing off her mask. She instantly began coughing on the horrid stench of the place. But she would not relent. The girl picked herself up and powered through. "I knew Estabon," she announced, "Julia, Michelle, Shamus, and Mrs. Rajado. They were real to me. They were my friends." Pauline paused to survey the crowd at large. Many of those people remained content to watch her from behind their devices rather than look up at the real, living person before them. It had never bothered Pauline so greatly as it did in that moment. She said, "And I for one believe their deaths were avoidable." She need not look far to find a wasted plastic bottle. One sat right beside the podium on a pile of broken chairs. Pauline knelt down to collect the easy example, stood, and held the bottle out before her so everyone could see. "It is time we seek a way to make a change."

CHAPTER 2 - POEMS FOR CHANGE

Like moths to a flame…

AO: What are moths?
ODOM: A classification of insects that lived on Earth
over two thousand years ago. They would come out
primarily at night and loved light and heat.
AO: Then why did they come out at night?
ODOM: Good question. That is precisely the reason why
butterflies were born.
AO: What are butterflies?
ODOM: I can show you after the lesson.

Like water flowing downhill, a movement had begun. Pauline's speech at the memorial ceremony was witnessed by millions of humans across the world – people like herself who had previously not realized how bad things had gotten. It seemed as though the population of Earth was at last prepared to take real, meaningful action to fix the garbage crisis. But how to do it? Who could possibly organize such a gigantic task? The politicians had been failing for the last five hundred years. And most environmental protection organizations had been disbanded due to lack of funding. It could not be anything like that, the movement required a figurehead – someone people could respect and believe in. The movement required Pauline Delgado. She would have to learn to climb the steps of greatness and combine humanity's cumulative interest in cleaning up the planet with a keen level of planning.

For days, young Pauline sat in her room searching for the key, formulating a plan, and writing poetry. Some of these poems were very simple like:

I am not whole until the Earth is whole.

Some were more direct like:

Why can we not pick up after ourselves?
Certainly that would start the trend.
Why can we not pick up after one another?
Surely that would prove our point.
Why can we not be cleaner creatures and produce less
    waste in the first place?
Definitely then we would not be in this mess.

AO: That's a poem?
ODOM: Most certainly. Poems can be clever and
    beautiful. Poems can be strange and mysterious. And
    sometimes poems can be quite blunt.
AO: Oh. I wanna write a poem.

Indeed, one poem in particular captured the minds and imaginations of Pauline's new followers. In it she said:

I am buried
In the mud
Crawling
Crawling
Through the mud
But it is not the mud that made me
That seeks to bury me
Farther
Farther
I descend beneath the mud
Until all I am
Is mud
And shit
And stench.
Do you too feel the mud
Pulling you down?
Do you feel the mud
Over your head?
We must dig up the mud
Or we will surely drown
We must dig up the mud
Or everything soon will become
Mud and silence.

When Pauline posted those words on her poetry app, many were listening. Many heard the call and helped the girl to rise through the ranks of celebrity. She appeared on television, on internet billboards, and social media sites stating messages of cleaning, recycling, ridding the world of waste. Even the politicians could not ignore Pauline any longer.

One day, Pauline was formally invited to meet the President of Brazil Superior. She instantly accepted the request and as the days passed by leading toward that event, she found sleep becoming a more and more difficult task each night. Often, Pauline would forgo even attempting to sleep since she knew sleep likely would not come. Instead, she would spend those nights awake in her room writing new verses and researching the possible answers to the Earth's many problems.

On one of those sleepless nights, Pauline noticed a news reel about the distant world of Adonis where the humans of the ark spacecraft, Papillon I had made their home. She thought about the lesson Mrs. Rajado had been attempting to teach on the day of the accident. And she remembered her question – "What about the other Papillons? Why doesn't our syllabus talk about them?" Pauline thought about Mrs. Rajado's answer, how Papillon II had failed. She knew that Papillon II was not the last of the massive ships in existence. So she searched and searched and from the depths of the internet she found hope.

CHAPTER 3 - THE NEXT PODIUM

Pauline waited at the event until her name was called. She felt a lump in her throat and a nervous sweat trickling down her back, but she also felt the frustration and anger that had lived within her ever since the walls caved in on her and her classmates. She could be aggressive and speak with purity to this crowd. After all, many of them were already on her side. And the ones that weren't soon would be. Stepping out into the strange light of the dais, Pauline approached the next podium. There actually were a lot of people at this event unlike the others where she had spoken. Most of those had been populated by internet viewers and local friends and family. This was the house of the President. This was big time.

She breathed in deeply as her eyes found President Torres sitting down among the group behind her. Briefly, Pauline wondered if that man was bored to be here. His eyes were on some device – likely internal, political documents… or maybe a speech – as a group of close confidants whispered in his ears. *State secrets?* Pauline wondered, *Or inside jokes?*

But then, for only a second, President Torres looked up and saw young Pauline staring back at him. He raised an eyebrow as if to say 'Bring it little girl.' Oh yes, Pauline would bring it to him. She would bring it to the whole entire country. Pauline smiled back and the President returned his eyes to his device. She wondered if the man understood what was about to happen. And before she knew it, she was standing at the podium, front and center before thousands of actual, living people. Her largest crowd by far.

She began: "Thank you, President Torres. Vice President Elano. Fellow speakers and listeners. Thank you for having me at this illustrious event. My name is Pauline Delgado and I survived the trash cave in at Canard Public High School three months ago."

AO: What's a month?
ODOM: Back when Earth had one complete moon, the people would calculate intermediate periods of time by the cycle of its orbit.

Pauline continued, "I have gained my status because of my poetry. I will read you one now.

"The Ark

The Ark passes through—
Through space and time.
It carries bodies to a distant world – It
does not carry their burdens. At least, we are to
presume it doesn't – not the physical hoards – just
the lifeforms. But one is lost and one is wasted – and
one has yet to learn its fate. We would like a world
without the hoards – we all would – we all agree.
The stench and undignified horizon line that
makes up our everyday—
We did not ask for this.
The first Arks ran from it.
But Arks are made to hold,
not be wasted
in
petty exercises.
The next Ark should take our
burdens from us– We need
not escape them—
They
simply
must
leave us in peace."

Pauline paused to see how the audience was responding. Their attentions were wrapt on her position. For the first time since the girl could remember, nobody in the crowd was looking at a phone or a tablet or any other device. They all watched her, gave their undivided attentions.

What a moment, Pauline thought before returning to her writing. "I speak, of course, about the Papillon mission. It was the last lesson my teacher, Mrs. Rajado ever tried to teach me. And I believe she must have known something before that crude pile of garbage crushed the life from her. I believe Papillon is the answer to this terrible problem." Pauline then turned around to see the President once more. "President Torres," she called to the man. He, unfortunately, had still been tinkering around on his device throughout her performance. But his eyes blinked up at hers like one caught in a trap. "Please would you join me at the podium," Pauline requested.

President Torres looked around awkwardly, but rose to his feet none-the-less. Pauline had known that he would. Who would refuse her at such a time?

"You are an interesting girl," President Torres griped, "never before has anyone summoned me in such a way and without warning." The man was rather sheepish all of a sudden, and the onlooking crowd was clearly more intrigued by Pauline's actions and words than the President's response. President Torres realized this after surveying the crowd and he tried to save face, remembering more or less what topic the girl was supposed to be speaking about from his daily briefing. "You have convinced me," he stated, not really knowing what it was he was agreeing to, "Yes. It is time we took charge of the sorry state of our lands. Tell me young one, what would you have us do to rid our world of this filth? How would you have us remove it?"

Smiling broadly so all could see, Pauline knew exactly what to say next. In fact, she had rehearsed for this moment as much as for the reading of her poem. "Well Mr. President," she said firmly into the microphone, "on the day of the accident, my teacher Mrs. Rajado was trying to teach us about the Papillon space missions. I have spent many hours researching these ark ships in the weeks since and I've discovered that you may have one still lying around collecting dust."

The President chuckled finding it hard to believe. But the look in this girl's eyes became deathly serious. "Lying around you say?" Torres was confused and slightly flustered. He turned from the dais to ask one of those advisors he had been chatting with earlier if they really did still have such a huge, expensive thing lying around from the previous regime. The advisor shrugged, looked to his tablet for a moment, and quickly returned his gaze to the President nodding in a manner that seemed to say 'I guess so.' Torres was nonplussed. How could he get himself out of this situation without having to commit huge sums of money? How could he save face before this crowd and this girl – he checked his phone to try and remember her name – Pauline Delgado. He would not forget it again. Returning to the podium, Torres said, "An interesting idea. And to where would this ark ship be traveling?"

"Well," began Pauline, "I think we could send it..." she paused to savor her victory. She had already bested the politician. He had expected nothing of her and she had won. Finally, she said, and without further hesitation, "I think we could send it into a neighboring sun. If that seems unrealistic, I understand. But we wouldn't want to negatively impact any other areas of space with our trash. A massive star could burn it up in no time flat."

President Torres had to be careful. He could not appear insensitive to this young survivor. All she was supposed to do was recite a poem. That's what Finniko had told him. But now that she had called him out, it would be a PR nightmare for the President to say 'No.' "Now Pauline," Torres tried to sound as intelligent as he knew how, "do you realize how much money has gone into the Papillon missions over the last thirty years?"

"Yes, Mr. President," replied the girl. "It's just a suggestion. But... if I may... you sent Papillon III into space with no destination in mind at all."

"That was my predecessor," Torres tried to deflect but recognized that the audience did not appreciate that answer. He pulled out his phone and punched at it in order to get quickly informed on the subject. "But yes. We had to test and recalibrate all of our systems in order to be certain that the tragedy of Papillon II would not be repeated."

"Well.." Said Pauline, "What did you have planned for Papillon IV?"

Torres peered back to his advisors and one of them actually got out of their seat, came up to the President, and whispered in his ear. Torres translated the whisper for the girl and the crowd to hear. "Yes, you are quite right Pauline. I've been advised that such a task could be taken up by this

Papillon IV without any loss to its currently planned mission." The man had lost and he knew it. All he could do was try and save face. "You are a very bright little girl."

"Little woman, thank you very much." Pauline held her head up high and the crowd cheered for the young woman's strength. She shook the President's hand as he gritted his teeth through a false smile. A group of photographers pealed onto the stage and snapped many photographs of the moment.

AO: Wow! Pauline really told him, didn't she?
ODOM: Yes. She was a truly remarkable being.

CHAPTER 4 - THE HARD PART

With that, the Papillon plan was set in motion. Alongside the Brazil Superior Space Program, people from all around the world came together to collect as much trash as they possibly could. Pauline formed a not-for-profit corporation – something very rarely done in Brazil Superior where they so frequently scoffed at the business minded ways of their neighbors on the northern continent. But Pauline had known she would need the protections of such an organization behind her, both as a spearhead for other nations to follow and as a shield of sorts from other more dubious messages that her home country's government might try to force upon her and her initiative. She called her new company *Papillon 4 Change* and promised a safe transition of waste onto the ark ship in collaboration with all governments across the world. No nation could deny the moral integrity that young Pauline represented, and for a time, many new and lasting alliances were born. It was finally time for all to come together and clean up the Earth.

In the first two days alone, *Papillon 4 Change* raised five times its estimated budget. Civilian teams were quickly disbursed across land and sea. It was hard labour, but for a good cause. And many people were willing to put a little hard work in so that their own children might enjoy the boon of a clean world the likes of which their own ancestors had not cared to provide.

Bi-weekly, Pauline would charter a boat out to the trash islands that floated freely throughout the vast oceans of her world with groups of volunteers in tow. Much footage would be collected during that time of the young woman getting wrist deep into the trash and coming up holding larger piles than she should have reasonably tried to carry by herself. She took these heaps and walked to the sides of the boats where nets and buckets would wait for drones to collect them. Those drones would fly the nets and buckets to a nearby launch port where small rockets would sit in waiting until they were filled to capacity. Once full, the rockets would shoot out into neighboring space where Papillon IV had long ago been constructed and simply lingered in waiting for its glorious new mission.

FIRST INTERLUDE

AO'S AMENITIES

Earth - Better Days

"For all intents and purpose," declared Odom as the projections dissipated, "this ends young Pauline Delgado's role in the story."

"Oh really?" Asked Ao, sullen at the words, "I really liked Pauline."

"Yes. So did I. But don't worry, her fingerprints will be on much of what is to come." Odom allowed the light in his library to change into something soothing and natural. "Are you hungry, Ao? Are you tired from your journey?"

Ao had forgotten about her own body during the course of the story. She said, "I guess so."

Odom's orb materialized before the girl. "Follow me," he said. And Ao followed him through the rows upon rows of computers. She realized now that these devices were far better organized than she had initially thought. They almost felt like pathways leading up the walls to some great focal point that she could not see, like the gyrus folds of a brain. Ao knew what a brain looked like. Greck had shown all the children an example back in Nikke of a simple surgery that could be performed to help anyone suffering from regular seizures. At the time, she had thought the presentation particularly disgusting, but the girl Greck had performed the surgery on had not experienced a single seizure since. She was a cool girl named Leen. She always told the best stories at the campfire. As Ao thought about Leen, she realized she was already missing her village of Nikke. She wondered if she would ever see that place again.

The orb turned a corner and a new door opened leading into a small, closet sized room. It had a tiny bed, perfectly suited for Ao's minimal stature, a table that could come down from the wall for eating off of, and a small potty and cleaning station for the girl so she would not become uncomfortable or dirty. The artificial sounds of droplets in a cave played for her and she realized she had to pee. "Can I use that potty right now?" She asked in a hurry.

"You may. This will be your room while you stay with me. You may use whichever amenities you wish."

Odom sounded kind, but then Ao became uncomfortable. "Will you… will you be watching me while I go?"

This time she was sure that Odom was laughing. He said, "I will only monitor your chemical samples to ensure you are in good health."

"You mean you're gonna look at my pee?" Ao asked awkwardly.

"And your poo, too," Odom replied. "But I will not watch you as you put them out. I promise."

"Then that's okay I guess." Ao approached the potty.

"Simply call my name when you are ready for me to return," Odom said kindly. Then his orb left the small room closing the door behind.

Ao finished peeing and hopped onto her new bed. It was a different sort than she was used to – more foamy and supportive. She had been used to mud and hay-packed sacks at sleep time. At present, Ao couldn't decide which she liked more. Sitting there, back against the wall, she studied the strange layout of her room. There was no wasted space. Every inch had a clear purpose. Again, she found herself wondering if she preferred this way of building things or the more free form hodgepodge blueprint of Nikke. But then, her tummy rumbled. She was hungry after all. "Odom," she called out. It took the orb a moment to return through the doorway.

"Yes, Ao," said Odom. "How can I help you?"

"I'm hungry," Ao licked her lips and rubbed her belly.

The orb floated along past the table which lowered into place beside the girl. "Indeed," he stated, "and what kind of food would you like to eat tonight?"

Ao had never been asked that before. "Egg?" She asked back, wondering the purpose of having to state the obvious to this orb.

"Egg." Odom became contemplative, "Yes, of course. And how would you like it prepared?"

Again, Ao was confused by the question. "In a pile?"

"Ah yes," Odom's voice became light then, almost tinny "The Nikke special. A pile of cattle bird scrambled eggs coming right up." Something turned on behind the wall – a deep humming sound – and then a shelf expanded horizontally forward from a hole that had not existed over the table a moment before. Within that shelf rested a pristine tupperware lunchbox. "Be careful while removing it," Odom cautioned, "the edges may still be hot." Ao reached into the shelf and carefully raised the lunchbox out placing it onto the table before her. It did not burn her fingers and she was grateful for that. "Go ahead," Odom was telling the girl, "open it."

She did. And there were her eggs. In a pile, just like she'd always had them. Ao took a bite. It tasted normal enough. She took another and another until all of the egg was gone.

Then Odom said, "By the way, Ao, this is a butterfly."

A projection formed in front of the doorway of a beautiful insect with bright, colorful wings.

"That's so pretty," said Ao.

"In times before, the moth would run into many issues" instructed the orb, "nighttime predators, lack of light and warmth, not so tasty food. They evolved into these butterflies so they might enjoy the sunlight and they developed marvelous colors and patterns along their wings in order to better blend in with the flowers of the world so daytime predators might leave them alone. Fortunately, the flowers offered a delicious nectar and butterflies became obsessed with that food."

Ao was noticeably surprised as Odom's presentation flew around in front of her. "Wait a minute," she said, "you mean the butterflies changed everything about their lives in order to get to eat tastier food?"

"Sort of," said Odom. "That is certainly a part of their story. Incidentally, the word Papillon that we have been studying so intently means butterfly in the French language."

"Wait, really?" Ao cried out, "That is so cool!"

"Yes, it is metaphorically a statement of mild temperature implying both fun and joy," Odom replied awkwardly.

But Ao was thinking about the food again. "So you're saying I could have chosen something different to eat other than eggs?"

"You could if you wanted to try something new," Odom agreed. "That can be a part of your education should you wish it."

"Okay," Ao contemplated out loud. "I'll try something different next time." And then the girl was yawning.

"Are you sleepy now, Ao?" Asked Odom.

"Yeah, I'm sleepy," said the girl. The lunchbox rolled back into the shelf, the shelf pushed into the wall, and the table closed on its own. Then the lights changed to create an atmosphere for better sleeping. Ao was already out before most of these tasks were done.

"Goodnight, Ao," Odom whispered sweetly, and quietly the orb left the room.

In the morning, Ao awoke with an awful dry mouth. Her body was not used to temperature controlled spaces. She leapt out of her bed and drank directly from her self cleaning station. After a long period of breath catching, she said, "Odom?"

The orb returned more quickly this time. "Good morning, Ao. Can I help you with something?"

"I think I'm ready to learn again," replied the girl.

"Excellent," the orb began humming. "Come with me."

Ao followed the orb out of her room and back through the winding rows of technology. The more she saw of the inside of the library, the more clearly she could decipher the patterns within the space. There were rows that led to other bedrooms similar to the one she was staying in. There were additional rows that instead pointed toward some other kinds of spaces – obviously larger than a closet. She wondered if Odom would ever show her those other wings. But, in short order, they arrived back in the same main library room where the orb had taken her the day before.

"How was your slumber, Ao?" Odom asked in a kindly voice.

"It was good, I think," she told him. "But when I woke up, I'd never been more thirsty in my entire life."

"Ah yes," Odom contemplated, "such things will happen as your body adjusts to the library. It is not a permanent issue, I assure you."

"Okay. That's fine I guess." Ao was still trying to get the grogginess out of her system, but she was also very curious. "Hey, Odom?"

"Yes, Ao?"

"Do you have other kids here?" She didn't exactly know why she had asked this particular question. Maybe seeing those paths to other rooms had gotten her going. Or maybe she just missed the campfire camaraderie of Nikke.

"I do," Odom said abruptly. "And several adults as well. You can meet them in time. They are all kind entities. I believe you will like them very much. But first, we should catch you up on your lesson. Are you ready to discuss what happened next with Pauline's ark ship?"

Ao's mind was swimming with a new excitement. She was going to meet some new friends... eventually. In order to do that, she would have to hear about someone other than Pauline Delgado which was frustrating. But, she was beginning to trust Odom more and more. She could wait a little longer to meet the others. "Okay. Yes, I'm ready."

The room transformed around her once again.

BOOK II

ELION TORRES

Earth - The Anthropocene Period

CHAPTER 1 - THE PRESIDENT, THE MAN

The President of Brazil Superior did not consider himself to be a bad person.

AO: Wait, we're talking about President Torres?
ODOM: That is correct, Ao.
AO: But why do we have to talk about him? He seemed like a real jerk.
ODOM: Yes. I understand why you would feel that way. Unfortunately, his story is particularly important to tell if we are to get to the place where we plan to be going.

His name was Elion Torres. As a youth, he had grown up watching futball and playing with broken toys – hand me downs from wealthier families' children. The piles of garbage had not been so terrible for him back then. At least, he had not noticed them and they were much easier to avoid than they would become by the time Pauline came around. As Elion Torres aged into a young adult, he witnessed his world shifting between meaningful forms of political strength. The super powers of old ceded away control before his very eyes. Nations once called the Russian Federation, the People's Republic of China, and the United States of America all dropped out of the world conquering game in favor of new trade concepts and transforming fiscal potentials. The former United States of America, for example, had collectively decided after much scrutiny and debate, to demonopolize into multiple, separate corporation nations in order to enhance productivity and advance new revenue and supply chains.

Elion Torres, the youth, watched as his country was allowed to thrive in a way the nation had previously not been able. The Federative Republic of Brazil evolved into the mighty Brazil Superior. The newly empowered country traded with the most powerful CEOs of the Demonopolized Corporate Nations of America for weapons, chemicals, and technology – including the necessary components to develop their own space program. Elion saw these changes occur over the course of three decades. And in that time, he got ideas, gained popularity with the political elites of his country, and was eventually seated in the House of the President. He had not gained his position because he was the best man for the job. He had simply learned how to make friends well. Of course, there are more important facets to being in charge of a nation than knowing how to make friends.

By the time Pauline became a force in the world picture, President Torres had already become bored with his post. Perhaps, that boredom was the beginning of the worst phase of Torres' life… though it would take the history books a very long time to recognize the man, Elion Torres, for the instigator of destruction that he really was.

AO: What do you mean by that?
ODOM: I will show you in short order.

The greatest threat to the nation of Brazil Superior at that time in Earth's history was not considered to be the overwhelming garbage on display in every crevasse of the land. Nor were the politicians of that country particularly worried about the rising sea levels that would eventually envelope more than half of all the dry land the world over. Such topics, to men like Elion Torres, had become passé – ugly – unavoidable, yet easily ignorable, eventual facts of life that had been handed down neglectfully from one generation to the next… an unbearable nightmare gift that was no longer worth worrying about. For men like Torres, it was far more popular to be concerned with the overall concept of boredom. If the population became bored, they might actually notice what was happening around them and demand some action that the members of the government believed they could neither plausibly form a solution to nor afford to pay for from their meager trillions of dollars budget. In this way, Elion Torres was simply the next in a long line of such pessimistic leaders. This does not make what the President did in the days to come any less terrible, but it is necessary to understand that he was not the only human to behave in this particular fashion.

For weeks, Pauline Delgado's Papillon plan seemed to thrive and flourish. And in that time, all reports of Elion Torres' behavior within the House of the President were of a joyful man who had found a new level of popularity and meaning. His political career could coast along on the Papillon achievement for as long as he remained in office. And, in a way, it did. The people of Brazil Superior would never learn what you are about to find out.

AO: What are you talking about Odom? You keep acting like something bad's gonna happen.

ODOM: Indeed. It happened long ago, Ao. And it was horrendous.

CHAPTER 2 - PROMISES, PROMISES

One day, an ordinary rocket filled with garbage ascended into the pocket of space where Papillon IV awaited its trash load. A drone collected the rocket's disgusting cargo and gently carried it the last stretch of the way to one of the space ark's many depository doors. The poor drone attempted to cram the garbage inside, but it would not fit. Papillon IV was too full for this rocket's load. And it would be too full for the next rocket's and the next after that. Within the course of only a few hours, Papillon IV could hardly even be seen behind the billions of tons of excess garbage still waiting to be loaded onboard.

AO: That doesn't sound good.
ODOM: I know. But this was still not the worst thing to have happened.
AO: Oh no. What's Torres gonna do?

The Earthlings had created so much waste that they could not fit it all aboard Papillon IV. When this revelation finally came to light, President Torres was called into the Brazil Superior War Room for a critical briefing with key members of his cabinet and staff. Those in attendance included the President, his son Elion Jr., his first advisor Finniko Extraordinaire, Vice President Likis Elano, and a panel of three scientists – Doctors Travathan, Warby, and Constantine – all specialists in their own respective fields.

AO: Why was Elion Jr. there?
ODOM: Nepotism, Ao. A failure of justice.

Finniko Extraordinaire led the proceedings – "Mr. President, if we are to continue heading this initiative, we will likely be asked to donate another Papillon ark ship to help carry the remaining excess trash."

On the monitors lining the walls of the War Room, images of islands of trash lingered in the middle of the ocean. Plastic bottles floated here and there with crabs and other creatures trapped inside. A whale was beached on the surface of the largest trash island. Its corpse rotted and alarmingly few animals were willing to approach the dead creature to pick at its bones.

"We don't have another ark ship to give. Do we?" That was the President talking. Since he had entered the room, he felt a terrible migraine coming on within the upper left chamber of his fore skull.

Doctor Travathan replied, "Not at this time, Mr. President."

"What about another government?" President Torres was intent on the idea of his own country not spending another dollar on the Papillon initiative. It didn't matter to him one bit that Papillon 4 Change might be capable of raising a substantial amount of those funds. After the initial gift of the last space ark, he had immediately resolved to be done with the project. No force on Earth could change the man's mind. He still felt the sting of his embarrassing defeat at the hands of the girl, Pauline. And his sense of pettiness was more powerful than his moral compass. "Couldn't India spare a vehicle of the necessary size?" Torres asked.

"I have been told," said Finniko after Doctor Constantine whispered into his ear, "the Indian Space Program has hit another snag with their latest attempt at moving off world. They do not anticipate building anything even close to the scale of a Papillon within the next decade."

President Torres placed the palm of his hand against his forehead where the ache was growing most prominent. "Haven't we done enough already?" He asked. "Why did I have to meet with that girl? Why *that* girl?" He was looking off toward the trash island with his one good eye. Pauline Delgado was there soaking her arms in a pile of garbage and carrying it to the boat as she was known to do. She had grown so tan and muscular since he had met her. In a way, Torres was becoming jealous because he had never been able to put on enough muscle mass to join the school futbol team as a child. And this girl was doing that without even trying. The President returned his attention to his advisors. "What are our options here?" He asked with aggression.

Each of the advisors looked to the others in turn. They behaved very awkwardly, peering down at their notes and clearing their throats.

After some time, and a plethora of whispers and nods between the bunch, Finniko Extraordinaire finally spoke up. "As I have said, we could begin building a new ark space craft."

"And how much does one of those cost?" Asked Torres thinking to himself that everyone he knew was a moron.

"Early estimates," Doctor Warby spoke up for the first time, "state a new Papillon would cost the tax payers upwards of two trillion dollars to manufacture."

Torres was not impressed by the assessment. He tapped his finger against his temple, accidentally worsening his headache. "What else have you got?" He asked like a broken record.

AO: What's a broken record?
ODOM: I will add it to your list.

Again, Finniko spoke for the group. "I believe this would be less popular, but we could pull out of the initiative altogether."

"That's obviously not an option," Torres slapped back. Why hadn't Finniko warned him better on the day? He wondered. Why was this task falling to him of all the Presidents in the history of the world?

"No," Finniko's eyes seemed to search the room for aide, "I shouldn't think so."

Catching wind of his advisors' combined malignancy, Torres decided to state the obvious. "So… either we bankrupt the country or we commit political suicide."

"That's not exactly how I would put it but…" Finniko trailed off when he saw the hateful look in the President's good eye.

Elion Torres was spitballing in his mind. He had done this kind of thing in the past so Finniko knew what it meant. Usually the President only behaved in this way when he hoped to destroy a political rival. At those times, the behavior seemed a wonder to behold… but on this occasion, Finniko felt that something was off. Whatever the President would say next was more likely to be travestying in nature rather than genuinely bold. The initiative to clean up the Earth was a good thing… and good for the President's polls. Finniko knew they should continue to try to be involved in the right way, yet he said nothing.

"How about this…" said the President, "now bare with me, okay? How about we… um… we latch the excess garbage together in space and create a rudimentary sort of garbage bag… a net… and we… attach it with like a tow line… to the back of Papillon IV. We save on funds and save face. What do you think?"

Finniko Extraordinaire was surprised by the President's idea. He wondered briefly if such a jury-rigging could work. But as he looked around at the three Doctors, he could see the shock in each of their eyes.

It was Doctor Travathan that tried to talk sense into the leader of Brazil Superior. "Excuse me sir," he said, "but it is very unlikely that a trash heap of this scale would remain wieldy enough to hold itself together across the distance of space."

"It doesn't have to make it across the entirety of space…" argued Elion Torres completely in ignorance of Pauline's earlier wish not to clutter up the universe in the process, "just to that neighboring star… uh, what was its name again?"

Doctor Constantine said, "Barnard's Star, sir."

"Barnard's Star! Exactly!" Shouted the President.

Barnard's Star was, at that time, a red dwarf star that hung in space about six light years from the planet Earth in a constellation known as Ophiuchus. As the fourth nearest known star to Earth, it had been decided by the initiative's planners to be at sufficient distance from the two known human worlds of Earth and Adonis without being too far for the ark ship's longevity to become a risk. Of course, such calculations did not – and never would – take into account the addition of a loose-mesh space-net tied to the back end of the craft with roughly the same mass and density as what had been stowed inside.

Only Doctor Travathan tried to argue. "Mr. President, I really need to make this clear to you… We don't want our trash spilling out all over the galaxy. That would be a PR nightmare."

But Torres would not relent. "Look," he said brusquely, "I need this off of my hands already. Just don't mention this little snag to the public and let's get on to other business."

"But Mr. President–" Doctor Travathan's final plea was never heard.

"I've said my piece." Elion Torres rose from his seat. He would never understand the true gravity of what he had just done. "Besides," he continued, already onto the next foolish thing, "I'm late for my lunch with the National Futbol Team."

Torres left the room happy to never speak of the matter again.

His advisors began to pack up their briefcases in silence.

Doctor Travathan sighed and said, "What a shame."

SECOND INTERLUDE

THE PROBLEM WITH PROBABILITIES

Earth - Better Days

"A shame indeed," said Odom – the image of the War Room still displayed around them. "This is a trend we see time and time again throughout history."

"As emotional beings," Ao repeated words she had heard an elder say back in Nikke, "we humans have a tendency to get lazy when a project no longer seems fun or easy."

Odom felt pride in that statement, "What an astute observation, Ao. Though it is not just an issue among your own species. Laziness has permeated across the many ages of this universe. And ignorance as well." Changing the projection to the constellations of space, Odom continued, "You see, there was an inherent problem in the concept of the Papillon mission. It assumed, and rather foolishly, that based on probabilities, no other living beings were likely to occupy any pockets of space within a one hundred thousand lightyear radius. But what can be classified as living? Far too frequently, the human species has misinterpreted their own data, often reading their probabilities in reverse or neglecting the base rate for prior probability altogether."

"I'm confused," said Ao scratching her head.

"My apologies," Odom chuckled. "It would seem I have just exemplified precisely the kind of mistake I am referring to. You see, Ao, you made such a very intellectual assessment of the human condition a moment ago that I nearly forgot I was speaking with a five-year-old who has yet to learn about the principals of probabilities in the first place."

"That's a lot of 'Ps'," Ao giggled out. She was having fun in the projection of stars listening to Odom talk himself in circles.

"It is," Odom laughed in reply. "You are a funny child, Ao."

Ao smiled and said, "Thank you."

Then, Odom had a fun thought. He formed up a representation of a television monitor floating in space before the girl like the beginning of an ancient episode of Rod Serling's The Twilight Zone. "Let us look away from Papillon for a moment to ponder a separate event on a planet known as Tharsis B in the Dumbell Nebula."

The Squid and the Clam Shell

The Nebula highlighted itself in the distance beyond the television. But on that little screen, a green, underwater world faded into view.

Tharsis B's one huge ocean was a strange but friendly looking place. Life there appeared particularly similar to an Earth suburb of the 1950s... only underwater... and the primary lifeforms were more squid-like in nature. One of those Squids lingered on the ocean floor counting out shells.

ODOM: The primary beings of this world had developed a primitive form of currency based on the shells they would accumulate while hunting lower lifeforms.

"Fifty three," said the Squid, counting its shells, "Fifty four... But I need fifty five shells to purchase my new Bipedal." The Squid looked up at a passing group of Bipedalers... other Squids riding around on floating bicycle-like contraptions. Then, the Squid noticed a Clam swimming by and grabbed the smaller animal with its long tongue.

"No no!" Squealed the Clam in a high-pitched, squeaky voice. "Please stop!"

But the Squid was already trying to scoop the Clam out from its shell. "Why should I?" Asked the Squid, "I need your shell to purchase my new Bipedal."

The Clam had an idea in that moment... it wondered if any other clams had thought of it before. "Well, I could lend it to you," said the still shelled critter, "but please don't take me out of it."

That stopped the Squid from trying to wrench the Clam from its home. "Really?" It asked, suddenly all mixed up inside, "I'd never thought of that before. But I don't know. Could I convince the owner of the Bipedal shop to take your shell with you still inside?"

"Hey," replied the Clam, "it's worth a shot."

Standing before the shop owner just a short while later, the Squid watched as its shells were counted out.

"Fifty three," said the owner, "Fifty four. And fifty five."

From the pile, the Clam gave the Squid a wink and the Squid said nothing to the shop owner about the still living creature in the currency.

"Pleasure doing business with you," said the owner.

"Likewise," replied the Squid as it collected its new Bipedal and left the shop.

Later that night, in the darkness of the locked Bipedal Shop, the Clam opened its eyes from within the pile of shells. It saw another shell there that looked familiar and wondered…

ODOM: *The problem was, the primary beings didn't realize that they were all living on borrowed currency.*

The Clam said, "Hey Chalky. You there?"

And another Clam named Chalky opened its eyes saying, "Here. Memphis, you there?"

A third Clam said, "I'm here."

And a fourth and fifth and sixth and seventh… Almost all of the shells opened their eyes.

The first Clam shouted, "This way my fellow shells! Let's move to greener pastures."

The shelled critters all swam to the door, unlocked it, and swam away leaving the register almost completely empty. Out in the open ocean, those Clams met up with thousands more of their species coming out of other neighboring shops. Together, they formed a great, streaming school that extended toward a beautiful luminescence far off in the distance.

ODOM: The primary beings had lied about their shells and one night, their economy literally got up and swam away.

Seemingly still floating in space within the library, Ao asked, "So what happened to them all?"

Odom replied, "The Squids fell into civil war. Their numbers dwindled and ultimately the Clams became the dominant form of life on that planet." Odom removed the projected television and continued, "There was a problem with how the Squids viewed probabilities. They assumed that leaving one Clam in its shell was not a big deal because it was simply one Clam. The Squids did not consider that if they were leaving a Clam alive, other Squids were probably leaving one alive as well."

"Killing is wrong," said Ao awkwardly.

"Yes, Ao," Odom agreed, "and so is lying. When making decisions for today, it is important to think about how they will affect others tomorrow."

Then Ao asked, "So how does this relate to our lesson on Papillon IV?"

"Do you understand what the President did wrong?" Odom replied with conviction.

"I think…" Ao tried to reason, "I think Torres wanted to be done… but the work wasn't finished."

"Yes. Good," said Odom. "Elion Torres wanted his hands washed clean of the garbage problem. Mind you, it was not a problem he had ever intended to tackle in the first place and he was ill prepared to deal with it or manage any new issues that might come up along the way. So, when the first major hurdle appeared along his path, he simply tripped over it because that was easier than trying to jump. And then he lied about it by omitting from the public forum that there ever had been a problem that required fixing."

"So the space net didn't work?" Ao asked, scratching her head again.

"No. It did not."

Papillon IV and its new net of towed garbage floated through space before Ao. The net rig looked so sloppy behind the space ark and every few moments, a piece of trash would escape its bind and settle into stillness – a trail of garbage leading all the way back to its source.

"So what happened next?" Ao asked staring morbidly into the garbage.

"Many things," said Odom. "The cleanup project did work at correcting the garbage problem, and, for about twenty years, the Earth seemed a better place to live. Pauline did get to enjoy the spoils of all of her hard work... until she reached middle age."

"Why only until middle age?" Perplexed, Ao felt herself getting nervous, for she had really liked Pauline Delgado. And even though it had all happened a long time ago, she really wanted a happy ending for the woman. "Did she die?"

Odom was silent for a while. "Of course," he seemed to whisper almost in another voice, "All mortal beings will die in time, Ao. You know this."

Ao began to cry.

"I know it is difficult to face the truth of mortality," Odom spoke louder, "but perhaps I can give you some solace. Pauline died of old age in a safe place surrounded by friends and family. She did not suffer. Before she died, she founded a community that continued to thrive even as the rest of the Earth fell victim to other disasters... Even as the wealthy fled to other worlds... rising sea levels were the start..."

"This was twenty years after Papillon IV?" Asked Ao.

"Yes," said Odom, "you are a good listener, Ao." Against the back wall where space did not have any representation of a Papillon or a planet, Odom brought up a visual of that version of twenty-years-later Earth. It swarmed with storm clouds and the moon was in pieces. "The humans destroyed their moon in a misguided attempt to harvest raw materials and calm the tides of an ocean that now spanned about ninety percent of the globe."

Ao had to ask, "How big had the ocean been before?"

"About seventy one percent of the globe had been covered in water before this point," said Odom.

"That's a big change," Ao whispered.

Odom understood the girl's surprise. "Many perished. Torres among them."

"How did he die, Odom?" Ao wondered, not knowing how to deal with this strange emotion of relief at the thought of the former President's demise.

"Not well I'm afraid," said Odom. "He may have been a misguided person, but even he should not have suffered in the way that he did."

"Can I see?" Ao did not know why she wanted to see the man die. But the urge was there.

"No," Odom replied abruptly. "I understand why you might wish for this, Ao. But it is not part of the lesson and it would not be good for your mental wellbeing to witness such a thing at your age."

"You showed me the kids in the school..." Ao whispered, suddenly perturbed.

"I did," said Odom. "It was necessary for the lesson. Torres' death is not and there is enough morbidity in our lives already... When you are older, Ao, I will give you the choice to see this moment within the context of a different lesson should his fate still appeal to you then. But be aware, even that will not give you satisfaction for the crime of which you have yet to fully understand. When the lesson is called for, okay?" Odom saw the sour look on Ao's face.

Still, she said, "Okay."

And Odom moved on. "Some time after the moon was destroyed, I was born."

This comment seemed to take the edge off for young Ao. She said, "I thought you were supposed to be without age."

"This is true," Odom answered, "but only half true."

"How can something be only half true, Odom?" Ao was obviously confused.

"I was born when the emotional learning of an aide computer's AI bonded with the advanced mind of an interdimensional being. Therefore, I was born in this universe at a particular moment in time, but likewise was not born at all as the other dimension exists outside the bindings of time. Do you understand?"

Ao's eyes were very big now. She was only five after all. Concepts of the fabric of space-time and dimensional relativity would not be within her wheelhouse for some years yet.

"Perhaps we should return to the lesson," said Odom feeling the youth's attention slipping.

"Yeah. Okay." Ao's eyes returned back normal and she let her breathing do the same.

BOOK III

ARIKO SEVENSON

Adonis - The Indigenous Age

CHAPTER 1 - THAT THING IN THE SKY

Sixty years had gone by since Papillon IV left Earth's orbit. And now it was entering the window of visibility to the planet Adonis.

AO: Sixty years? Why did it take so long to get there?
ODOM: Because of the garbage net, the Brazil Superior
Space Program decided it would be safer if the
space ark embarked at limited propulsion. For
obvious reasons, this would slow down the entire
process creating more opportunities for something
to go wrong.

Ariko Sevenson was a daughter of one of the few families on Adonis capable of operating the remaining pods from the Papillon I mission that landed almost ninety years before. She was a third generation Adonian now referred to rather forcefully by the government as 'indigenous' as if the classification would make the human species' dominance and claim over the new world fact and not simply hubris. Ariko was a stout, strong woman, top of her class at the Academy of Foresight and Stability – Adonis' primary developmental commission for world planning. And she happened to be the first Adonian of note to spot the massive thing entering visibility in the night sky.

How it happened was on the night of Versa – the 113th day in the Adonian calendar. Ariko was studying atmospheric sight lines to ensure a newly conceptualized skyscraper would not interfere with the visibility of any astronomical activity of note. The Adonian people were very fond of the stars and the world's lack of over-construction and intentional low lighting made it an ideal place for galactic viewings. In fact, while we are on the subject of over-construction, it is noteworthy that as of that particular moment in history, the only manmade structures of the world at all had been harvested directly from the hull of Papillon I. This new skyscraper would be the first building to cut into the Adonian land in a real, meaningful way, and as such, its plans had been under deliberation by the Academy of Foresight and Stability for more than a decade.

Now, on the night of Versa the 113th, Ariko Sevenson spotted a large anomaly coming from the Sol system. "What is that thing in the sky?" She asked aloud as she stared through her telescope. She took pictures and rushed out to find Professor Twelfmin.

Twelfmin was in her office preparing a lecture for Eco the 121st day. She was working on a section about recycling broken stone from what would be the world's first quarry in the event an excavation did not go as impeccably as they hoped. The Adonian peoples were real sticklers for having tiers of foresight protocols in place for almost everything. They did not wish to become a repeat of their former world of Earth.

Ariko Sevenson came rushing in saying, "Professor Twelfmin. Professor Twelfmin." The girl was clearly out of breath and had to collect herself. The Professor gave her the time she needed. "It's… something new… in the sky. I saw it on the eastern horizon coming from the direction of the Sol system."

Professor Twelfmin lowered her lecture papers and raised an eyebrow. "It's coming from Earth?" She asked. "What does it look like, Sevenson?"

"I don't know to be honest," said Ariko. "If I didn't know any better, I'd say it was a Papillon. But they wouldn't be that crazy, would they? To send another ark ship to our world would be…"

"No," said Twelfmin. "We must not assume anything yet. We must retrieve more data."

Pulling up her three telescopic pictures, Ariko remarked, "It looks bigger than a Papillon actually."

Twelfmin peered over the images with intensity, "You're right, Sevenson. We shall have to get a closer look at this thing. How long would you say until it is in range of your family's pod?"

"You'd like me to go up?" Asked Ariko in astonishment.

"Yes," and the Professor repeated, "How long?"

"A day… maybe two?"

"Let's aim for just the one, shall we?" Twelfmin was adamant – excited even.

Ariko nodded profusely, "Of course, Professor. I won't let you down."

AO: Torres didn't tell Adonis about Papillon IV?

ODOM: He did not inform them that it would be headed their way, no. And by the time this all came about, the Earth was covered in those terrible storms and communication between the two worlds was impossible.

CHAPTER 2 - WALKING IN SPACE

Climbing into the ninety-year-old pod, Ariko reflected on the possible meaning of this – it was serendipitous that she had been the one to spot the object – she who was only one of five Adonians with the requisite DNA to operate the one-man pod and perform any kind of space walk or other maneuver. She found herself meditating as she calculated the odds… five hundred thousand to one. Ariko Sevenson got to be that one. She had always wanted to take the pod up on an actual mission. This was her chance.

Self assured, she plugged her fists into the activation holes. The small spacecraft's interface lit up as though it had been driven only yesterday. In truth, it had been closer to five years since Ariko had last taken it out for a 'joy ride.' She breathed a deep sigh of relief and spoke into her mic, "All systems seem to be in good working order on first inspection. Running a diagnostic now."

"Good, Sevenson," Twelfmin replied all the way from the lab. "Keep me posted."

Ariko fiddled with the controls and the computer spoke up mimicking the voice of an ancient astronaut, "Welcome aboard Ariko Sevenson. It has been a long time."

"Too long," Ariko replied back. "I missed you, SUCO."

ODOM: SUCO was short for – Scientific Union Computer Operator. It was an artificial intelligence similar to the ones that built the foundations of my programming.

AO: So SUCO is like your family?

ODOM: Yes. I suppose it is.

"All diagnostics have come back in good condition," said SUCO.

"Excellent," replied Ariko. "Twelfmin," she said into the mic, "I'm ready for takeoff."

To which Professor Twelfmin answered, "You have the green light."

Ariko activated SUCO's flight parameters, the pod lights dimmed, and the engines shot into gear. Everything lifted off the ground in Ariko's immediate vicinity and she peered out through her three monitors as they showed her visuals of the world Adonis getting smaller below her. The pod was engineered in such a way that she could ride up out of the atmosphere and her equilibrium would never be able to tell that she had left the ground.

"I am in space now," Ariko said, assured by the small ship's vitals that this, in fact, was the case.

SUCO became philosophical then, "It is a strange feeling to be going backwards after all of this time." It was speaking, of course, about the path taken by the first Papillon in order to reach this world. SUCO's algorithms had witnessed that trip firsthand and it had a very reliable memory.

"So this is the same path you travelled all those years ago?" Asked Ariko.

"Yes," said the computer, "only in reverse."

"Can you tell me," Ariko wondered, "if the object we fly towards is following that original Papillon path as well?"

The old computer had to take some time to calculate. Then it said, "It is not. Though it is remarkably similar."

"How do you mean SUCO?" Asked the woman.

"It is moving about ten times slower, and its projected path forms a straight line into deep space beyond us. The necessary ellipse to bring the object to Adonis proper does not seem to exist."

The computer's assessment gave Ariko some semblance of relief. Adonis was a large enough world, but given the current infrastructure, the people who lived there could not afford to welcome another large batch of human settlers.

"I can confirm," said SUCO in a rather befuddled manner, "that the object is, in fact, a Papillon."

Ariko's heart nearly popped out of her chest at that. "Did you hear what SUCO just said Professor?"

"I did," Twelfmin's voice responded from back on the planet's surface. "SUCO," she asked, "can you confirm to us that there is life on board that vessel?"

SUCO performed a life scan. "I can confirm that, but for the exception of a small colony of garden variety insects and arachnids, there are, in fact, no intelligent lifeforms on board."

"Odd," thought Ariko, "why send a Papillon all this way without anyone on it?"

SUCO then stated, "I can also report that there is an object of immense size being towed behind this Papillon. It is filled primarily with scraps of undefined materials."

"Perhaps they have sent us additional building supplies so we don't need to harvest our own land yet," said Professor Twelfmin with a newfound sense of optimism.

Ariko didn't know what to think. The Professor's words sounded so unlike the Earth she had been told about. "SUCO," she asked the computer, "if there is no recorded life onboard, what's inside the hull?"

Scanning the ark ship again, SUCO replied, "It is difficult to register. I sense similar kinds of material as in the towed object. I also sense nuclear waste byproducts of a harshly degraded nature."

Twelfmin was concerned. "Is Ariko in danger of succumbing to radiation poisoning?" she asked.

"Doubtful," answered SUCO. "The pod is well padded."

"Would she be in danger if she stepped out of the pod in a space suit?" Twelfmin asked further.

SUCO's systems calibrated to the new request. "I should say, Ariko Sevenson would not be in any more danger than on any other spacewalk. The radiation is substantially less than that of a distant star."

"What do you want me to do, professor?" Ariko was curious.

"I'd like for you to find out if anything within the second object on the back could be considered useful to our construction initiatives down here," said the older woman.

"Yes, M'am." Methodically, Ariko strapped herself into her space suit, always in waiting for the passenger within the cushions of the pilot chair. Her helmet came down last and fit snuggly over the braced collar buckle. "I'll go out right now."

"Beautiful, Ariko," Twelfmin relayed.

Ariko pulled a small lever within the arm holster and the pod split open like a Pac-Man mouth.

She had never been on a spacewalk before and the immensity of it all was rather shocking without the monitors to give her a sense of up and down and scale. And that was just space. Above her head, the shadow of the new Papillon trotted along. It was... breathtaking from this viewpoint. "Come on, SUCO," Ariko said bravely having reestablished her sense of direction across the body of the ship. SUCO held her to the pod with an emergency oxygen and harness line, so the two had to move together. The woman and the computer flew quickly past the massive stingray head of the ark – where the people would have been housed – and down to the thinner, though occasionally bulbous, rolling body where the majority of technical functions were performed.

They passed the primary propulsion systems. "Strange," said SUCO, "that these have not been set to a higher power level."

"Agreed," said Ariko noting that almost no light was emitting from the engines.

"It must be a precaution due to the nature of the other object," the computer continued.

And then, Ariko saw it… the net. At first, it was confusing for her to look at the thing. She tried to sort out the various knots and shapes that bulged out here and there across its face. But nothing on first inspection made any sense at all.

"What do you see, Sevenson?" The Professor was asking after all of the girl's silence.

"It's…" Ariko didn't know how to describe it, so she said, "It's nothing."

"Nothing?" Twelfmin felt a spiteful taste on her tongue.

"It's…" then Ariko's eyes came into focus. She was close enough to see the old popsicle packaging and broken down, petroleum built, washing machines, the old car bumpers and cosmetic applicators… "It's trash, Professor. It's just trash."

Twelfmin smacked her palm to her face. She was defeated by the moment. "Those Earthlings…"

"I have more to report," said SUCO rather abruptly.

"Go ahead," said Ariko.

"It would seem the object is leaking."

"Of course it is," said Twelfmin, down below. "They just had to clutter up our space too."

AO: Odom?
ODOM; Yes, Ao?

AO: If the people of Adonis came from Earth only a century before, aren't they equally as responsible for creating all of that garbage in the first place?

ODOM: Yes, Ao. It has been a topic of great discussion amongst the intelligent lifeforms of our universe. But the people of Adonis have never been particularly receptive to such a message.

AO: That's lame.

ODOM: We are in agreement of that, Ao.

Professor Twelfmin did not want to put Ariko in any further danger for what she now believed to be a lost cause. She said, "Sevenson, please collect a small sample from the point of the leak and get back to Adoni Firma."

"Yes, M'am." Ariko spotted an old tire floating away from the massive net. She wrapped her arm through the hole at the center and pulled the piece of rubber back into her pod which closed around her and returned her safely to the planet's surface.

CHAPTER 3 - SAVE OUR SPACE

The tire sat on a desk, staring back at the women, mocking them. Ariko had dropped the useless piece of space junk there in Twelfmin's office, washed herself clean as was protocol, then returned to see the professor had already cored her sample from the rubber, tested its traits, and come to the obvious conclusion that the people of Adonis could gain nothing from another attempt at harvesting the Earth's old trash now spilling out at a rate of three items per hour across their pristine skyline.

"I don't understand why they would do this," said the Professor in a state of shock.

"Me either," said Ariko, "but I can't say I'm surprised. Everything I've ever heard about the people of Earth leads back to the same two traits — they are wasteful and they are selfish."

"True. But this," Twelfmin continued to postulate, "this is too much. We were meant to escape all of this. They've ruined everything, Sevenson."

Ariko sighed. She did not like to see her Professor in this state. "Might I recommend," she said, "that we take an action, Professor, so that this is not the case?"

Twelfmin took a seat and poured two cups of cured aquavit from a decanter. Ariko joined her and they drank the clear yellow liquid. Then the professor asked, "What did you have in mind?"

"We could operate the five remaining pods," Ariko told her, "get all of The Numbers together and push the trash back into the net – sew it up so the leak no longer persists anywhere near our sector of space. From what I could see, the hole was not so great. With all five of our pods, I bet we could complete the task in a single afternoon."

Twelfmin poured another round of drink and smiled. "I'd like to review the data again first. But it's not a bad idea, Sevenson. If everything looks as you've said, I'll put the word out to The Numbers."

"Excelsior!" Said Ariko lifting the aquavit to her lips once more.

"Proste!" Twelfmin replied and did the same.

AO: What is aquavit?

ODOM: A Scandinavian spirit distilled from the likes of the caraway or dill plant. Its name is derived from the Latin 'Aqua Vitae' meaning 'Water of Life.' The people of Papillon I took great care to import the necessary components to Adonis throughout their years journey almost losing the crops on three separate instances.

The Numbers assembled, the heads of household of the twelve pure families of Adonis. Those who had been ranking officers along the Papillon I mission would forever be represented as born leaders in the original governing body of Adonis. It was a broken system as much as many have been before it. An oligarchy plain and simple. But it did not fail Ariko Sevenson in this instance. She would one day be on that board of leaders after her mother passed and she was treated with greater esteem than Professor Twelfmin ever would be given her lower number ranking of twelve. Some would go so far as to call the eleventh and twelfth families only 'Numbers' in name. But that is a tale for a different time.

Ariko's five pod mission was given the green light. No one on Adonis wanted all of that garbage hindering their view of space beyond. So the five youths (Ariko among them) capable of operating the SUCO pods were called upon within the hour. The mission was labeled "Save Our Space." The words referring only to the space directly within visibility of Adonis itself.

For four hours, the pods worked as a team to assemble all the garbage they could find, stuff it back into the net behind Papillon IV from where the leak had emanated, and eventually seal up that tear. In the eyes of The Numbers the mission was a complete success and Ariko Sevenson would be named a hero of that world. She would even be honored with the renaming of the day Leto the 115th to Ariko the 115th — or Cleanup Day.

Meanwhile, as the people of Adonis celebrated, Papillon IV simply carried on leaving their sector of space in peace but presenting a genuine danger to another, as yet undiscovered planet.

> *AO: So the Adonians just swept Papillon IV under the rug?*
>
> *ODOM: Correct, Ao. They did not see it as their problem or their responsibility to dig any deeper. They thought that simply by sewing up one tear another was neither likely to form nor anything that they would ever have to think about again. And again, those living at that time would never know the difference.*

THIRD INTERLUDE

A NEW FRIEND

Earth - Better Days

Ao looked perturbed. She said, "I thought I was supposed to like Ariko Sevenson."

"Do you dislike her?" Odom asked removing the projections from view so the library could be seen once again around the girl.

"I mean," Ao contemplated, "she only did the bare minimum. Didn't think about anyone but those directly around her. And got a whole bunch of praise for just playing around in space for a couple of days. I guess I don't know how to feel about all that."

"Indeed," said Odom, "the context will become clearer with additional lessons."

"Okay," said Ao, "but I'm hungry. Is it meal time?"

Odom's orb appeared before her and said, "Of course. Shall I lead the way?"

"I think," replied Ao, "I can find my own way back if that's okay." She wanted to feel like she could make her own choices for a little while.

The orb allowed it. So Ao got up from her seat and began walking once again through those strange halls of technology. This time she really tried to remember the look of each device as she passed. The orb only followed as she went saying nothing until the girl seemed more receptive to its words.

Ao found the door to her quarters and went inside leaving an opening large enough for Odom to join her. She sat on the bed and the table descended from the wall without the need for a request. Then, Ao asked, "Can I have a cup of water? I'm thirsty again."

This time the cup skated out from a hole in the wall already full. Ao began to drink and Odom told her, "It is surprising to me that you require so much liquid water, Ao."

The girl stopped her drinking briefly to ask, "Why's that?"

"Cattle Bird eggs are a genetically enhanced super food," explained the computer, "artificially made so nutritious that most humans no longer need acquire their hydration from the natural liquid… It is one of the reasons the people of Nikke are so fond of them."

"Oh," replied Ao, "I just like the way water feels against my teeth." She placed the empty cup down on the table. It skated away and returned fully replenished within seconds. "Thanks," Ao smiled. "What should I eat, Odom?"

Odom's old programming retraced the gamut of popular food items throughout Earth's history. He settled on the number one item, synthesized and cooked the protein, and presented it before the girl saying, "This is called a cheeseburger. You may lift the whole item from the surrounding bread with your bare hands and bite into it sideways so you can taste all of its components at the same time."

Ao stared at the strange food with a frown. But she did as Odom instructed and found the sensation of chewing the sandwich surprisingly pleasant.

Odom projected an old analogue record player in the air for her as she ate. "By the way, this is a broken record." The vinyl laid flat and spun but the sound did not progress past a jolting, scratching sound.

"Why does it keep making that terrible noise?" Asked Ao with a full bite of beef in her mouth.

"Because it is broken," replied Odom. The computer raised the vinyl vertically away from the needle of the player, presented the scratched section so Ao could see, then filled in the small abrasion. He layed the large disc back down and allowed it to play an old, lethargic tune — like floating through the sky with no wind or turbulence to shake the listener.

"This is really weird," Ao spoke about the burger, "but yummy. Why don't we eat this in Nikke, Odom?"

"It is made from the muscles and fats of the bovine species."

Ao nearly choked, "This was an animal?"

"Traditionally, yes," instructed Odom, "but fear not Ao. As with your Cattle Bird eggs, this cheeseburger is fully synthesized. Like you said earlier, 'Killing is wrong.'"

Regardless, Ao didn't know if she wanted to keep eating. The idea of chewing on a piece of dead animal meat really ruffled her. She put the remaining quarter of beef down and said, "I think I have to poo now, Odom."

"Understood."

The orb cleaned up quickly and left the room, the vinyl still playing as Ao approached her toilet. She sat there for nearly ten minutes, the guitar lazily plucking all that while until — seemingly out of nowhere — a wispy man's voice began to sing in a language she did not understand. It was beautiful, but angry. Melancholy and brutal all at the same time. Delicate as a stained glass window but then rough like the rust on the vehicle out in that entry space where she came in the day before. Ao was enthralled by the mood of it. She had never heard anything quite like it before. She listened to all twenty six minutes of the track and when it ended there was a new sort of swiping click on repeat. This was different from the broken sound of before and Ao recognized that the record had ended and would not start again unless some unknown action was taken. She flushed the toilet, washed herself clean, and left the room to return to the main library.

As Ao approached the central hub where Odom had done the majority of his teaching, she realized that someone else was sitting there waiting for her. It was one of those rock people. She was used to their kind back at Nikke so the visual of this one did not surprise her so much as the fact that there was anyone in the room in the first place.

"Hello?" Ao said cautiously as she surveyed the older creature.

The rock person had actually been dozing there in Ao's learning place and it jolted awake at the word. "Hi. Hello. I'm sorry I must have taken a nap. It tends to happen more and more when you get to be my age," said the creature.

Ao noticed that its crystalline, craggy skin did look more weathered and dusty than she was used to seeing from the others back at home. And one of its arms was substantially smaller than the other, which was funny to the little girl. "How old are you?" She asked.

"Now that's quite a rude question to ask someone you've only just met," replied the rock person. "You wouldn't rather know my name or what it is I'm doing here or anything a little less touchy than that?"

"Yeah, I do want to know about all of that," answered Ao trying to save face before the stranger. "I just thought…"

The old creature saw that it had made things rather awkward for the girl, so it changed its tone from grumpy to apologetic. "That's alright. That's fine. I did not come here to scold you, young lady. I came on the behest of Odom. My name is Syk'Ry. And I am six hundred and twenty-two years young."

"Six hundred…" Ao was incredulous.

"…and twenty-two. Yes," answered Syk'Ry matter-of-factly.

Shaking her mind clear of the extreme age of this Syk'Ry, Ao said, "Why did Odom ask you to come here? Actually, where is Odom?"

"I am here," replied the super computer. "I extended an invitation to Syk'Ry because they had expressed interest in revisiting our next lesson for scholarly purposes. The timing was ideal. And I believe you hoped to meet some of the others who have been housing and learning here as well. Therefore, the situation seemed a win-win according to my subsystems."

"Oh," said the girl.

"Is it alright that I sit in on your lesson, young one?" Syk'Ry asked.

"Okay, I guess," said Ao.

"Your name is Ao?" The rock person asked further.

"Yeah." Ao felt a little shy.

Then Syk'Ry added, "I've heard about you." And smiled gently.

"You have?" She didn't know why, but somehow Ao didn't think that was a good thing. She decided to come clean, "I was in trouble back in Nikke."

"Yes. I am aware," said Syk'Ry. "But that's no matter. You are here now and you are learning. That is perhaps the best thing any among us can hope to do when they've made a mistake."

"It was..." Ao didn't know how to respond, "I didn't mean to."

"It's quite alright," Syk'Ry said gently. "I think you're a good girl, Ao. Based on everything Odom has told me, you have been a very attentive pupil."

"Thanks, I guess." That was more of a whisper. Ao felt all bristly on her skin. Embarrassed that someone else had been made aware of her present detention. She looked away from Syk'Ry for a moment and said, "Odom, that song you played me... it seemed really sad, but I couldn't exactly understand the words."

"Indeed," said Odom. "It is the tale of an Earth based band from the mid to late nineteen hundreds. Their front man left the band when confronted by an agent with the prospect of a solo career filled with fame and money. But then the band became very popular while the front man's solo career floundered. One day, the front man showed up at a rehearsal, sick and awkward. He behaved as though he had never left. But, of course, he had. His old friends barely recognized him anymore."

"My goodness," said Syk'Ry. "You played her *Shine On You Crazy Diamond*, Odom? That's a bit heavy handed, wouldn't you say?"

"I simply thought she would enjoy the song," replied the computer.

Syk'Ry turned their attention back to the girl. "You must have really pushed someone's buttons to get that kind of treatment from Odom here. He's usually a great deal more easygoing with his students than all that. What exactly did you get yourself into, Ao?"

Again, Ao didn't know what to say. She just hung her head and started to cry.

"I'm sorry, I'm sorry," said Syk'Ry. "Really, it's alright. You don't have to tell me. I know that you want to be a good person at heart, isn't that right?"

Ao nodded yes through her tears.

Odom intervened asking, "Are you alright, Ao?"

She nodded her head again, her tears beginning to dry.

"I'd like to begin the lesson," offered the computer, "if you're feeling better."

Ao wiped her eyes and tried not to frown. "I'm okay."

"Yes?" Odom asked one more time. "Then let's begin."

BOOK IV

FA'MICA

Po'Pito - Gelatinum and the Great Period of Adjustment

CHAPTER 1 - SEPARATIONS

It took Papillon IV more than five hundred years to reach its final destination, Barnard's Star. Au'Rok to the beings of the rogue planet Po'Pito.

AO: Five Hundred Years?
ODOM: The exact year of arrival was thirteen billion five hundred eighty-two million sixty-three thousand nine hundred and seventy-five.

At that time, Po'Pito was a world of silicone gelatin known as Gelatinum. It was a rogue planet which means it did not technically hold a consistent orbit through any one solar system. Hurtling through space, it simply happened to be passing by the red dwarf star, Au'Rok at the time of Papillon IV's arrival.

SYK'RY: Tell her about the lifeforms on Po'Pito please.
ODOM: Ah yes. That is the correct way to begin telling this story.

There were four thousand some odd beings living on Po'Pito at that time. Large, silicone based, gelatinous slug creatures. They fed off of the moss-like ground cover called drallum that easily grew across the soft surface of the world. And everybody knew everybody else... It was not a terribly large planet, but a paradise for those who resided there. The Po'Pitians wanted for nothing and death and turmoil were very rare concepts.

The image of the planet came to life then. Slugs moved slowly across the landscape.

"Morning Fa'Mica!" Said one of those silicone slugs to another.

"And a lovely morning to you, Chi'Chi!" Fa'Mica hollered back to the other. "How grows your family today?"

The first, more youthful slug called Chi'Chi looked to both of its arms and then backward at its similarly shaped tail. "I've still got all of my appendages accounted for unfortunately," it said with a frown.

Regardless, they both began to laugh. Chi'Chi's separation would come in time.

"Just keep trying there," Fa'Mica offered with kindness in their voice. "I know we could all use a few more Chi'Chi's in our lives."

AO: Wait, I'm confused. What are they talking about, Odom?

ODOM: Hmmm. It is a difficult thing to explain. You see, young Ao, on the planet Po'Pito in the year thirteen billion five hundred eighty-two million sixty-three thousand nine hundred and seventy-five, the primary life forms had evolved to give birth through a form of cellular division… something akin to the Earth process known as mitosis.

AO: Mitosis?

ODOM: When two cells split into equal copies. Let me see, where is it?

The projection of Po'Pito began to leap around in time. Fa'Mica and Chi'Chi first moved in reverse and then forward in their timeline until Chi'Chi's right arm had swelled to double its original size.

SYK'RY: Chi'Chi had an arm… and then they didn't.

Chi'Chi's swollen arm suddenly fell off. At first, the slug looked shocked by the event, but then the arm stood up. It had a face and it looked like a smaller copy of Chi'Chi. They both smiled and danced for joy.

SYK'RY: Then they were best friends.

AO: So the Po'Pitians wanted to lose their limbs?

ODOM: That is correct.

AO: Okay.

The Po'Pito slug beings lived extraordinarily long lives… thousands and thousands of years for some. And they could genetically pass certain memories along to their children, so in a way, they never really died. Still, Po'Pito was a simple planet. With extended life and wisdom, their species had come to the conclusion that less was more. Desire little and your needs will often be met. Care for the world around you and you can learn to be fulfilled by those around you who show similar care for your space – your kin. In this way, the Po'Pito managed to have plenty and want for little. They never felt a need to get anywhere in a hurry, because the entire planet was a welcoming home to all. But then, one day, the garbage bomb came.

CHAPTER 2 - THE GARBAGE BOMB

Papillon IV rolled through space. Its net had once again sprung a leak after the clean up mission off of Adonis. And for those many lethargic, crawling years, garbage had been leaving a trail behind the ark ship, littering the emptiness of space with ancient Earth waste. It arrived in the vicinity of Barnard's Star in the year previously listed and, by that time, the hole in the net was becoming a constantly tearing thing. Perhaps a quarter of the mass that had been held within the net remained and, unfortunately, that all dumped as it came within the gravitational influence of the planet Po'Pito.

AO: Oh no.

The garbage fell in droves toward the rogue planet's surface splashing into the smooth, gushy gelatin silicone like thousands of meteors striking all at once. Some few Po'Pito slugs were struck and killed by the garbage during those first cruel hours. But most of the species survived to face the even more terrifying period to come.

Fa'Mica, one of those many survivors, had always been a particularly lazy old slug. They would enjoy the spoils of drallum anywhere they could find them and, when rest was necessary, they would simply find a below surface air bubble and allow themselves to sink down into a cozy slumber pocket there. On this first day of the garbage bomb, they had been sleeping in such a hole, but were awoken by the rumblings of the impacts. Fa'Mica pulled themself up to the surface to see the peculiar falling materials and noticed that quite a few piles had already landed around them. In truth, Fa'Mica had been very fortunate that they had not been struck in their slumber bubble, for that would have meant certain death. And for some reason, a great deal of the mess had specifically clumped in their immediate vicinity. It was a narrow miss for the slug. Yet, unfortunately, this fact alluded Fa'Mica to begin with. They did not feel threatened at all yet by the bizarre event. They had never in all their thousands of years witnessed anything quite like the garbage bomb. So, rather than behave in a fearful manner, Fa'Mica chose instead to inspect these new piles of mass bleeding slowly into the gelatin surface.

They approached a blackened, charred item that had only just defrosted from the cold of deep space – a pile of cheap plastics that oozed into one another to make a whole heap of formless mess. If Fa'Mica had the need of a nose previously, perhaps they would have smelled the strange chemical composition that boiled within that plastic and chosen to leave it where they found it. But alas, they did not have such a sense and felt no fear of the stuff… so they ate from the pile of grabage as did so many others thinking it a new source of food. They did not yet understand the nature of the poison they willingly imbibed.

Back above the world, Papillon IV was completing its mission. It flew past Po'Pito and smashed directly into Barnard's Star with all of the other well sealed garbage incinerating along with its hull. The last moment of visibility from the ark ship was strange indeed. It melted away into just another molten lake on the red dwarf's surface. And then, the nuclear waste within ignited sending an immense solar flare blasting out and lashing at Po'Pito more than two hundred million miles away in a matter of about forty-five minutes. Like a gravitational grappling hook, the residual flare pulled at the mass of the rogue world and changed its trajectory – forcing it closer to the star and toward the very inner limits of any sustainable goldilocks zone.

CHAPTER 3 - THE HARDENING

Po'Pito rumbled terribly as the solar flare ripped the world from its rightful place in space. The slugs felt the shockwaves passing through the gelatinum surface. But Fa'Mica and the others like them who had already decided to eat from the scorched trash heaps hardly noticed that aspect of the environmental disaster. They were instead distracted by harsh feelings working their way through their digestive tracts. Fa'Mica began to change colors, the strange Earth chemicals interacting roughly with their own physical composition.

All around them, the garbage was beginning to sink into the gelatinum fabric of the planet, seating into the surface and lingering there like fruit in jello. Again, Fa'Mica did not see this, for the slug being was already beginning to harden – a bulky, crystalline shell forming along their body.

AO: That looks familiar. Syk'Ry, is that…?
SYK'RY: Yes, Ao. These gelatinous slugs are the same
species as myself and the rock peoples you know of
today. The harshness of the garbage caused a series
of chemical reactions and biological transformations

within my people to the point that we solidified into the entities you see now. We… hardened.

Not only did the slugs of Po'Pito harden, the gelatinum on the surface went through a similar transformation – locking Fa'Mica and the others out from their precious slumber bubbles just underneath. To make matters worse, the solar flare created by Papillon IV affected the orbital trajectory of Po'Pito to such a degree that the sun became enlarged across the planet's horizon. Au'Rok's rays became harsh and unforgiving to whichever side of the planet was exposed. It is worth noting for our purposes that a day on Po'Pito after the solar flare could last for as long as two Earth Years, and a night the same. Fortunately, the side of the world the majority of the species inhabited was pulled into night at first, so it took some time for the Po'Pitians to truly gain an understanding of their new circumstances.

Fa'Mica spent countless hours mourning the loss of their precious slumber bubbles. They would tumble along the now slate-like crust of the world trying desperately to recreate their former slug crawl to no avail. Their body ached and spasmed against its limb joints which could not seem to get used to this new form. Often, Fa'Mica would be found by their friends and relatives roving the wastelands, crying crude silicate from their many orifices, and seeking out some comfortable deposit of soft ground that simply did not exist. They did not sleep that whole night long.

AO: They didn't sleep? Was the night really two whole years, Odom?

ODOM: I'm afraid so.

AO: I can't imagine not sleeping for one day let alone two years. They must have been so tired.

SYK'RY: May you and I never feel so tired as those first rock people did.

When the end of the first Po'Pitian night finally did arrive, the former slugs were once again taken by surprise. The sun did rise — suddenly massive in the sky. Au'Rok sent its rays of burning radiation across the land remelting the surface into an unlivable nightmare-scape of thick, bubbling tar. In this new, terrible heat the Po'Pitians would melt — but they would not return to slug form — they would not turn into anything at all. If they melted all the way, they would simply cease to exist. They would die.

AO: How did they make it through that?

SYK'RY: Fa'Mica.

It is funny to consider that the laziest of this particular species could become so resourceful when the worst imaginable outcome was in sight. Fa'Mica saw their relatives closest to the visible horizon melt into puddles of nothing. They saw the tar ocean pressing toward them. And they sought — as they always did — to find their slumber bubble so they could sleep until all of their woes and worries went away. Feeling along the hard slate crust with their slowly melting hands, Fa'Mica appeared to be sweating – but that was simply a symptom of the melting process. "I know I can do something with this," Fa'Mica said to themself as they pressed against a spot they knew had previously housed one of those subterranean pockets. "Come on, Fa'Mica! Think! Think!"

And with each 'Think!' Fa'Mica smacked their hands against the crust a little harder. Each time their hands made contact, they pushed the slate a little further down until a cave-like hole burst open beneath them. Their eyes alighted with joy and they raised their head up to see their sweating Po'Pitian relatives in the distance.

"Everyone!" Fa'Mica called out to them with all of their might, "Come look!"

CHAPTER 4 - HOLES IN THE GROUND

The crowd of desperate Po'Pitians surrounded Fa'Mica as they presented their discovery. The lone slumber bubble was just the right size to house one of their numbers and possibly shield them from Au'Rok's cruel light. But would it protect the rock people from the developing tar as well?

"If we hide down here," said Fa'Mica, "we may not have to melt away and perish!"

Chi'Chi's nascent arm shouted, "Hooray!"

Other Po'Pitians responded in kind to the hopeful news. But then, their survival instincts kicked in for the first time in the history of their species… since such an instinct had never been particularly necessary in the past and the slug forms had not had to test them, it instantly became clear to everyone that they were not of particular use to this danger. The crowd had all at once attempted to cram themselves into Fa'Mica's lone slumber bubble.

Fa'Mica was completely buried beneath the pile shouting, "Wait wait!" against the mob. And the hole was obviously not big enough for everyone. They made a huge pile that stuck high up out of the ground.

Someone asked from halfway down, "Hey what's the deal?"

In their new rock form, Fa'Mica was able to survive the pressure of all of those bodies and push their way out of the pile. "Everyone!" They announced – the tar encroaching on the site more and more rapidly – "We've got to learn to make these holes for ourselves! And quick!"

Chi'Chi's arm pulled itself from the pile and declared, "But some of us are too small!"

"So we need to learn," Fa'Mica was realizing everything in that one moment. They really wanted to get into their hole and get some much needed slumber as fast as possible now that they had finally uncovered one again. "We need to learn to work together and take care of those who cannot take care of themselves as well." They patted Chi'Chi's arm on its little head and continued, "We need to dig bigger. Now if you'll all get down from that silly pile, I'll show you how I did it. I'll teach you how to burrow."

At first, the occupants of the pile seemed dumbfounded. Was Fa'Mica of all people really becoming the voice of reason for their kind? Slowly, the rock people pulled themselves away from one another and reformed a circle around Fa'Mica and the hole in the ground. And Fa'Mica did show them how they had broken through the surface over a preexisting slumber bubble. Together, the rock people learned how to burrow into the slowly softening crust in order to form much needed shelter from the harsh sun. Some Po'Pitians were born naturals at the process of cracking and scooping deeper and deeper into the heart of the land while others could hardly manage to scrape the surface. So, in an odd sort of way, Fa'Mica also developed the planet's first public works project.

These larger holes in the ground would become the Po'Pitians' subterranean dwellings any time Au'Rok showed its terrible face. At first, that was every two Earth years and the new way of life on that once rogue planet seemed sustainable. The rock people learned to dream and they developed nocturnal habits so the sun's rays would not harm them in that particular way again.

Finally, Fa'Mica was able to get some sleep. But this was only one problem solved. One of many.

FOURTH INTERLUDE

FILLING IN THE BLANKS

Earth - Better Days

Syk'Ry was watching Ao as the lights of the library returned to normal. They asked, "What did you think of Fa'Mica's lesson, child?"

Ao had to quickly review everything she had just seen to try and sort out what it might have meant to this rock person before responding – "I guess they had a really hard time. I can't imagine what it must have felt like to completely transform like that after being so used to a different body. I wonder if it hurt real bad. I feel bad for Chi'Chi's arm not being strong enough to dig for itself, but I'm happy the sun didn't melt everybody." Then Ao paused to try and see if she had gotten everything Syk'Ry might have wanted to hear. They were still just sitting there looking at her – calm but with intent. So Ao added, "I guess I wanted to get to know Fa'Mica a bit more. Odom kept saying that they were lazy, but I guess I can't really agree with that without seeing more examples of their laziness in other parts of their life."

"I see," said Syk'Ry. "I ask because I helped Odom to fill in gaps of this particular story."

"Gaps?" Ao asked.

Odom spoke up at that, "The entity without time that makes up a primary component of my being does not have complete access to the days of gelatinum on the world of Po'Pito. I can see many things on my own, but from time to time I do require an aide such as Syk'Ry here to fill in the blanks of my memory within this universe."

"So," said Ao, "Syk'Ry helped you to write Fa'Mica's story."

"That is correct," replied the computer.

Syk'Ry added, "I am certain that some of my additions were not without bias, though I did try to be as historically accurate as I knew how. Your notes will help us to make the necessary revisions. You, being so young and of human descent, are an excellent example of the kind of individual we wish most to impart this information to — hopefully in an understandable and exciting manner."

Ao sent the side of her mouth to each cheek in a back and forth of uncertainty. She asked, "Did my answers help?"

"They were very insightful," said Odom.

And Syk'Ry added, "It was important for us to see what things stuck with you and what things might have been missing. Odom and I will seek out aspects of my family memory that, in the future, may better reflect Fa'Mica's usual habits."

"Your family memory?" Ao asked.

"I am a descendent of Fa'Mica," replied Syk'Ry. "Therefore, I have access to some of their memories passed down over the generations. You see, like Chi'Chi's arm in the story, us limbs remember."

Ao took that statement to heart. It made her feel good to know that someone of Fa'Mica's bloodline... slug line?... whatever — family tree had survived into her own time. But then her recent education got the better of her sense of sentimentality and she had to ask, "Hey, Syk'Ry. One thing is bothering me... What did all the Po'Pitians eat after the hardening? Was that drallum stuff still around or...?"

"That's a good question, Ao," Syk'Ry replied.

And Odom said, "We have added food studies to her lesson syllabus since she comes from a community that does not offer a larger perspective on the subject."

"Oh? Very good." Syk'Ry considered Ao's question humming along with their thoughts as they did so. Eventually they found the right memory from Fa'Mica's life. "Odom, would you please present us with a projection of Gelatinum Po'Pito on that wall there?" They nodded to the place where the Twilight Zone television had appeared earlier, though Ao wondered if the rock person had known about that particular presentation as she was coming to realize that her own lesson plan was one of a kind and tailor made specifically to her.

Odom projected the base content of Gelatinum Po'Pito as Syk'Ry had requested.

Then the rock person said, "Please add Fa'Mica to that place there by the clump of drallum resting against that lump of silicate."

Somehow Odom found the correct drallum patch amidst what Ao saw as an entire field of drallum. In truth, nothing about Gelatinum Po'Pito looked to have any kind of visible landmark to the young girl's untrained eyes. Regardless, Fa'Mica as a slug stood in that place and Syk'Ry seemed pleased by the placement.

Syk'Ry spoke and Fa'Mica performed the correct actions to their words, "When we were slugs on Po'Pito, drallum — a moss like filament that would seep up from the pores of the gelatinum surface — was easy to come by. Easy fodder for all and none would go hungry. In the context of the greater universe, our ecosystem was extremely simple — a duo culture that formed out of a sort of necessity for the planet. You see, Po'Pito as a world liked its squishy gelatinous quality – and I honestly do believe it thought and felt as we all did before the garbage bomb. So that being said, in order for Po'Pito to remain in a state of constant gelatinum before Papillon IV, my people would eat the drallum the planet supplied us, our innards would process the mossy substance without destroying it... we would warm it and churn it into an even softer byproduct that would then seep back down into the planet to help power its core... then the byproduct produced by the core would again seep back up for us to eat in an endless cycle."

"Wait," Ao had to stop Syk'Ry, "you're saying Po'Pito was alive?"

Odom answered the girl, "Many worlds are alive, Ao. Even your Earth is living in a way. But this is a very large subject to tangent into at this time."

Ao looked around awkwardly. She suddenly felt as though she knew very little about the workings of the universe and it humbled her.

"Indeed," Syk'Ry continued, "thus it was an even greater tragedy when gelatinum was ended on Po'Pito. For, in truth, this meant the planet had died."

"That's terrible!" Ao shouted out. She wanted to cry.

"It is," said Syk'Ry. "My people were very sad when they realized what had happened. But all things do end in time. We have learned to accept this simple fact. When the garbage bomb came and polluted our world, Fa'Mica and the others ate from its litter and transformed as you have already witnessed. What Odom did not express in the previous lecture was the interdependence the Po'Pitians then had to develop with that trash."

"What's that supposed to mean?" Ao asked, a new anger building within her.

The image of Fa'Mica had transformed by now into its hardened rock person form, and it struggled to crawl toward a nearby heap of stinking garbage. Syk'Ry answered, "It means, with the death of the planet so went all of the drallum. With the loss of the drallum, all Po'Pitians were forced instead to eat whatever else was around. Whatever else was around consisted primarily of the Earthling garbage. Our people had to eat Earth's garbage to stay alive."

Ao felt sick. She wished she had never asked that question. "Garbage is gross," she said aloud.

"Yes, I agree," Syk'Ry responded — unhurt by the remark. "But it was all we had. It was fortunate that we did not require more sustenance than a few mineral molecules to sustain ourselves, and once that garbage had worked its way through our digestive systems, it broke down into a far more malleable material again. It was a good question you asked, Ao. A lesson Odom and I had not discussed teaching before. But now that I think on it, this is information I believe will come very much in handy over the course of your next several lessons."

Fa'Mica was walking away from a pile of plasticized trash they had just pooped out.

Ao was holding her nose even though there was no olfactory aspect to the video.

Odom asked, "Shall we carry on then?"

And Ao answered, "I'm getting kind of tired, but maybe I can do one more today. I don't really wanna end on that note."

Odom paused the image of Fa'Mica and propelled it further backward in time. Then the super computer expanded the projection to surround them as he had done so many times before.

BOOK V

CHI'CHI

Po'Pito - Gelatinum and the Great Period of Adjustment

CHAPTER 1 - THE OTHER ARM

In discussing Chi'Chi of Po'Pito, we must go back a few celestial years in time from where we ended our last lesson. The garbage bomb had just come and Chi'Chi, like so many others, had swallowed a whole heap of trash by themself not knowing that the food would change them. They grew crystalline shell formations along their body until they ultimately fluxed into the more modern rock person the Po'Pitians would eventually become. The unfortunate situation with Chi'Chi was that they were still deeply into their separation cycle. Yes, one arm had come loose and formed into a new entity before crystallization had occurred, but the other had plumped in its own right, and now instead of releasing from its once gelatinous progenitor, it would have to contend with a hardening of its own.

Chi'Chi watched that one plumped arm for a half a night. They watched it plump and plump. It had grown a face, but the face remained closed all that time. The arm did not seem capable of moving or speaking on its own. "Come on little buddy," they would say. But there was never any response.

The first arm came to greet them during that time. It asked Chi'Chi, "Do you think it will make it?"

To which Chi'Chi replied sadly, "I… don't think so."

As a slug, the Po'Pitian had worked so hard to eat enough drallum when they knew they were becoming close to a proper separation. Before the garbage bomb, one could expect to develop a full family of four between self, arm, arm, and tail. After the garbage bomb, one could not expect to accomplish any such thing. Chi'Chi had been fortunate to separate the first arm before the incident. But the other one still clung to them.

Seemingly overnight, a once strong and viable species could no longer reproduce…

AO: That's so sad. Is this story ever gonna stop being sad you guys?

ODOM: It is sad, yes. But it is also very important that you gain this information, Ao.

AO: But I don't like to be sad.

ODOM: No. Few beings in this universe enjoy that emotion. But we all feel it for a reason.

SYK'RY: Yes. Even Odom feels sadness.

AO: He does?

ODOM: I do. I see much of what occurs across time and space deserving of sorrow and sadness. It affects me as it affects you. And it makes me sad now to know that you are feeling so.

AO: I'm sorry, Odom. I didn't mean to make you feel sad too.

ODOM: It's quite alright.

AO: Okay, I'm ready to listen some more. I'll be good.

Unfortunately for Chi'Chi, they had not come up with any answers in the long night before Au'Rok came and tarred the land. They had to journey into their new underground home carrying a still attached arm that was becoming too large for their body. They would moan and groan and shirk their digging duties due to the great discomfort they experienced on a regular basis.

All the while, the rest of the rock people were burrowing out new and interesting subterranean spaces where the tar drips could not reach them – where they could gather and share each other's company – where they could spend time alone if they so desired. The Po'Pitians were building a city that would become a proper home during the long daytime cycles. But Chi'Chi was missing out on the joys of those successes. Their burdensome still born arm was all that occupied their thoughts during that first night and day.

CHAPTER 2 - PROCESSING GRIEF

By the time the first long day had ended, Chi'Chi had closed themself off to all of the others in their own solitary cavern. So it was a great surprise to everyone that as a team of surveyors returned from an early aboveground mission, Chi'Chi had climbed the steps of the first slumber bubble and stood there awaiting Fa'Mica and their first, now alienated arm.

"Fa'Mica..." Chi'Chi said to the group as a whole, not even looking up to see their estranged relative there.

From the back of the survey team, Fa'Mica pressed themself forward. "Chi'Chi!" They called in reply, "My good friend, what can I do for you today?" Chi'Chi's behavior seemed both erratic and shy. They did not know how to say what they meant nor how to mean what they said. So Fa'Mica added onto their initial words of friendship. "Come come! No need to hide your worries from us." Fa'Mica tried to point out the arm in the crowd so Chi'Chi would notice, but the burdened Po'Pitian was too wrapped up in their own struggles.

"I... it's this arm," Chi'Chi said with a terrible wail as they tried and failed to raise the appendage. "It should have split off long before this nightfall. And now I fear it never will. Still it grows and weighs me down… and… it does not speak or show me fondness."

Chi'Chi's other arm watched desperately from the crowd. All they wanted in the world was to have their friend back – to feel a part of a family again. But the disconnect of the parent was still too great.

"I have spoken with several others throughout the burrows," Chi'Chi continued their strange speech, "and have found that anyone else who was preparing for separation before the crisis has had the same issue. There are dozens of us who find ourselves weighed down by our own bodies with no aide to help us through to salvation. If…" their words broke apart in their mouth, "if this carries on… I worry that our species may never again bare children."

"Hm," said Fa'Mica trying very hard not to think about their next meal or nap, "this problem is more troubling than the last. We must think, Chi'Chi. That is how I was able to teach myself to burrow… creative thinking."

AO: Is that really what Fa'Mica said?

SYK'RY: In fact, yes. Fa'Mica had developed something of a rather large ego since their sole success with burrowing. They had all but forgotten that others had ever considered them lazy back in the days of the slug.

AO: But they weren't really thinking when they broke that first hole in the ground were they?

ODOM: This depends on our definition of the term, Ao. One might be processing a thought in the depths of their mind and not know that they had figured out the solution until the moment of reckoning is before them. In this way, Fa'Mica had been performing a kind of rational, creative thinking. And the distinction between that and perhaps a simple survivalist luck does not make a great deal of difference as far as Fa'Mica is concerned. Whether they had truly implemented creative thinking mechanics in their burrowing process or not, they were the only Po'Pitian to develop a solution to stave off Au'Rok in the necessary time to save the species.

Chi'Chi and the group of surveyors returned to the caverns below the surface and contemplated their plight. Chi'Chi asked, "And how does one go about performing this 'Creative Thinking?'"

To which Fa'Mica replied, "For me, first I stroke my chin..." they performed that action and the next, "then I sigh... hmmm."

Chi'Chi and the others echoed the sound. But as Chi'Chi raised their swollen arm to their chin, they found it to be too large and cumbersome to reach its destination. The Po'Pitian fell over and the oversized appendage cracked against the ground on impact. "Ouch!" Chi'Chi yelled.

"Oh my! Let me help you there, Chi'Chi!" Fa'Mica quickly came to their aide hoping they hadn't caused irreparable harm to the grieving parent. As Fa'Mica helped Chi'Chi back to standing, the swollen arm remained lying on the ground, half buried in a small hole there, standing on its own like a small stone tree.

It had finally separated and Chi'Chi looked to their newly vacated shoulder and the standing arm with surprise. "My arm!" They declared, "It's gone!"

"Hooray Chi'Chi!" Shouted Fa'Mica hoping the rest of the group believed they had meant for this very thing to happen. "That's one portion of the problem solved. How do you feel?"

Chi'Chi tested their range of motion. "Light... nimble..." they said, "I feel like my old self again... physically that is." Then their gaze turned wholly to the standing arm. Chi'Chi went through a host of new emotions as they looked upon the separated limb. First, relief. And that sense of relief swelled within them and they began to lubricate their craggy pores with crying discontent for the next feeling to take Chi'Chi was the one called guilt. They felt guilty that they had been relieved. Love and sadness, sorrow and regret. They tried to bargain with themself for many hours and the crowd of surveyors dwindled. Fa'Mica even left having solved the great problem of infected-limb-initis.

But Chi'Chi's arm remained after the others had gone watching their parent and their unmoving sibling, wondering for a long while if they could help either one of them... wondering if Chi'Chi would even notice that they were there – feeling their own guilt that they had desired their parent's attention so even as Chi'Chi struggled through this terrible experience. Why had one arm survived while the other became an obelisk half buried in a trench in a cavern deep underground?

CHAPTER 3 - KEEPER OF THE GARDEN

Chi'Chi watched their stillborn limb without food or sleep for all of that nighttime…

AO: They didn't eat or sleep for two whole years?
ODOM: That's correct. And even longer as the story is
      told.
AO: Ugh.

And their first arm stayed with them most of that time trying to help Chi'Chi even as they refused that help. The arm would drag food down and plop it beside the parent. They would try to talk to Chi'Chi to help them through their sadness. But rarely did the parent reply and when they did the word they said was almost always "No."

Still, the arm did not wish to give up on Chi'Chi. And they knew it was not healthy for them to stay in that place wasting away as well. So they devised a plan to keep Chi'Chi from ever having to be lonely. They could, at the very least, help in that small way.

The arm traversed the subterranean cave systems seeking out other Po'Pitians who were going through a similar plight to Chi'Chi's. Those in separation who could not separate. Those whose limbs would not animate in order to enter the realm of consciousness with the rest of their people. The arm would find these other Po'Pitians and bring them, one by one, to the place where their progenitor mourned. Once there, they would show those others how Fa'Mica had thought. And just as Chi'Chi had done that first time, the others would lose their balance and the ailing limb would break off in the cavern's soil.

In this way, that site became something of a field of obelisks – colloquially referred to as The Garden. It was Po'Pito's first medical establishment, and in its heyday, it was a beautiful and tragic place to behold.

After three long days and nights of this, Chi'Chi's first arm said to the parent, "I'm tired Chi'Chi…"

And Chi'Chi finally responded to their first born, "But still we have no solution to the greater problem at hand. We've removed these infected limbs and stimulated new growth." Indeed, Chi'Chi's shoulder sockets had begun to grow two new arm stubs that would one day become fully functioning appendages for the Po'Pitian so long as they remained attached. "But," Chi'Chi continued solemnly, "we still have no answer to this lack of new children among our species."

"Yes, Chi'Chi," said the arm both relieved to hear their parent's voice and exhausted by their request. "I'm afraid we won't be able to solve this issue without a proper rest. You have not slept in four nights, Chi'Chi. Why don't you get some sleep. I would like very much to do the same."

"I cannot leave them," Chi'Chi replied. "These limbs are my charge and I am their keeper. I will remain here at The Garden so long as they need me."

Chi'Chi's arm had known in their heart that such an answer would be coming. Still, it did not change the great sadness that they felt in that moment. They would never be Chi'Chi's focus. They would have to come to terms with that reality. And one day, they would. But in the meantime, they did as they said they would – they left the field of limbs behind, found a slumber bubble cavern suited to their minimal stature, and slept there. All the while, Chi'Chi remained where she had been – Keeper of the Garden. Warden of those who had not awoken. Carer for those who could not care for themselves. It would become a position of honor for Po'Pitians across the ages.

FIFTH INTERLUDE

A BAD SLEEP

Earth - Better Days

Like some pious, religious leader, Chi'Chi's face hung there in the aether for a long time. Ao stared back at it, agog. "Is that… does it just end like that?"

"Chi'Chi's tale is an odd one, I admit," said Syk'Ry, "but no more so than many of your Earth stories."

Syk'Ry patted at their smaller arm with their larger one and it occurred to Ao that they must have gone through that same terrible discomfort before separating like Chi'Chi and all the others had done. She felt a sadness at that but did not think it polite to ask the Po'Pitian directly about what was likely a stillborn child. So she grunted and said, "That's not really the kind of story I was hoping to end on before bed."

"My apologies," Odom remarked. "It was simply the next story to be told."

"I know," Ao hung her head and tried to hold back a yawn, but the deep breath forced its way through the girl all the same. She was sad, tired, and angry. A very bad combination indeed.

"Are you ready for bed, Ao?" Odom asked in a kindly tone.

"I am tired, but…" Her words would not come.

"But what?" Syk'Ry asked.

"Do you guys realize what this story is doing to me?" Ao rubbed at her eyes, suddenly miserable.

Odom's orb appeared before Ao and Syk'Ry and said, "I hope it is informing you greatly of our collective universal history, Ao. That is my sole ambition."

"No," said Ao with frustration, "it's pissing me off!" It was a phrase she had heard Leen say several times back in Nikke. It seemed fitting.

Syk'Ry ogled the orb which appeared to look back in the direction of the rock person. They were sharing some unspoken form of communication which merely angered the human in the room even further.

"Don't do that!" Ao shouted. She was now becoming very cranky. "Don't pretend like I'm not here! That's how Chi'Chi treated her arm! I feel so bad for that arm! Why did Chi'Chi have to ignore it? Wasn't the other one already a lost cause?! That's not a way for a parent to act toward its child!"

Then Syk'Ry returned their gaze to the girl and bored it into Ao's heart. Of course, she cried almost immediately.

"I'm sorry Syk'Ry," Ao spurted out through her drooling tears, "I'm sorry my stupid species ever came into existence. I'm sorry. I'm sorry." Her words descended into gravelly, sobbing mutterings. She was only five after all.

So the rock person rose from their seat and lifted Ao in their larger arm. "Show me the way please, Odom." The orb directed Syk'Ry to Ao's chamber where they lowered the girl, already snoring, into her bed. "Goodnight, Ao," Syk'Ry said solemnly. "I am sorry to have caused you this pain." And the rock person left the little girl to her fit filled dreams.

In that state of slumber, Ao experienced several small nightmares. She imagined herself on the world of Po'Pito during Gelatinum living with the slugs. And then Au'Rok was before her, melting her. She imagined Elion Torres' mocking laughter coming from that distant star. She could even see where the solar flare reached out and tried to grab at her forming into the former President's lazy hand. Ao felt that fiery hand grasp her around her waist, and then a thousand more such hands reached across space to grasp the other slugs there. Together, they melted into the soil under foot.

Ao had never melted before. She found she did not enjoy the experience. Like everything around her was falling – slipping away from her. No. Now she herself was falling, collapsing through the aeons of time, watching space swirling around her, wrapping her in its unimaginably massive maw. It was all terribly disorienting – dizzying and puke worthy.

Suddenly, she felt she was back in Nikke. Only it wasn't Nikke at all, not really. The buildings were all wrong, the soil was covered in pounds and pounds of garbage, and the old community structure was crumbling under a terrible trash heap that seemed to make up the exterior walls of the place. She heard Sid there crying out for her. "Ao!' Howled her youngest sibling, "Don't leave me here, Ao!" And for some reason, Ao quietly repeated her hate filled words from that day… those ones that had gotten her in trouble in the first place – "You little, goose bellied, horn-eyed runt…" though the worlds felt strange on her tongue this time. She tried to run toward the building then as it collapsed around her crying sibling, but her feet were still melted and she couldn't seem to get any closer. She knew she couldn't save Sid. She knew she had done the wrong thing and she felt like she would never be able to make it right. Finally, the building did collapse… it just looked like a junkyard, like there had never been any structure there worth even looking for. Sid's whispering voice floated up to her through the junk saying, "Ao… don't leave me here, Ao." But then the voice began to sound more like Syk'Ry's…

Ao woke up in a cold sweat. She was alone in her chamber. "Syk'Ry?" She said. But Syk'Ry was not there. So Ao got up out of her bed very slowly. Her head hurt a little and she was fairly certain that this was not a normal time for her to be awake. She opened her chamber door and looked out on the halls of the inner computer maze. "Odom?" She spoke across the threshold. She saw some crude form of light drip down from high above the computer shelves – something she had never noticed before – and then the orb appeared in front of her.

"Ao," said Odom even more gently than usual, "is everything alright? You had yourself quite the fit earlier."

"I wanna talk to Syk'Ry," said Ao as she rubbed the sleep from her eyes. "I owe them an apology."

The orb hummed awkwardly. "I am sorry, Ao. But Syk'Ry has gone."

"Gone?" Ao did not understand.

"Syk'Ry had an important matter to attend to. They will likely pass through Nikke on their journey however." Odom watched the girl with curiosity. "Would you like me to submit a message to the elders there on your behalf? Syk'Ry and they are old friends. They would not withhold your words should you have something to tell them."

Ao didn't know what to think. Why would Syk'Ry leave so suddenly? She had only met the rock person yesterday, but already she felt a deep need for their approval. "No," said the girl, "I wanna tell them myself. I have to apologize for..." What was she apologizing for again? She knew it was important and she had to stop to think.

Odom chimed in again, "I know you must be confused, Ao. Our lessons are confusing. But Syk'Ry does know you are sorry. You told them some five times before you cried yourself to sleep."

"No, I need to tell them." Ao was still in a fit. Her junk sleep was bleeding into this waking moment and she still did not know how to calm herself down. "Syk'Ry!" She shouted brushing past the orb and out into the hallway. "Syk'Ry!" She began to run, to search for the way back out to the vine and chaparral road. She wanted to chase down her friend and apologize for all the wrongs her species had done to them. But she quickly got lost within the maze of technology.

'Ao," Odom tried to warn her, "Syk'Ry has gone. But they will not be gone forever."

The girl ignored the orb that followed behind her. Where was the exit? She couldn't remember how to get out. She was breathing too hard. Swiftly, she turned a corner and then she saw a door. Without another thought she ran to it.

"Wait, Ao!" Odom cried out, "Don't open that!"

It was the first time Odom had ever been truly stern with the human, but she ignored the warning all the same. She shoved the door open and stepped into another chamber. Odd. It was larger than her own sleeping quarters, but not dissimilar. There was a bed, a lowered kneeling table that had enough room to rest on the ground with plenty of space between it and the other furniture, and a familiar looking washing station. That's where she spotted the other being. It stared back at her in clear surprise. She had never seen anything like it, smooth bluish skin and a sort of beak on its face though it was clearly not a bird. Its joints implied that it liked to run across wide swaths of land and climb strange terrain on all four of its limbs. The creature hunched and moved toward the girl. And Ao realized that she was not breathing at all in this room. Something was wrong and she couldn't even try to pull the air into her lungs. Her eyes rolled back into her head and she felt the force of the creature as it shoved her wholly out of the chamber and briskly slammed the door closed in her face.

Fortunately, her breath returned to her back out in the hallway. But her throat hurt and she was struggling to focus. She realized that Odom was speaking to her but she could not understand the words at first. She just looked around stupefied. Then finally, the volume returned.

"That is not how we behave here, Ao," Odom was telling her. "You could have died. It is so fortunate that you did not accidentally step into a water chamber or a Nexus reactor, but I must have you understand that these doors are here for your protection. Do you hear me?"

Ao looked up at the orb coyly. "What was that thing?"

Odom's orb quaked with anger and then calmed itself. "That 'thing' is a member of the Eakress species. An intelligent life form from a distant galaxy." Odom tried to warm his tone again, but he was very upset. Still, he would always be honest to his charges. It was his will and purpose to understand and help them in any way he could. "I owe the Eakress in much the same fashion that you feel you owe Syk'Ry and the Po'Pitians, Ao. This one's name translates to 'Right Angle.' She is here to learn from me as I must learn from her."

Ao sat down right there in the hall next to the alien's door. "Right Angle?" She said, "What kind of a name is that?"

"She is a scientist," replied Odom. "It is fitting."

"It's silly to be called after a shape." Ao was beginning to lighten.

"It is silly," Odom replied, "to be named with two vowels and no consonants."

Ao didn't understand the statement, but she laughed anyway. Her breath was back to normal and she was glad for that. "What happened to me in there, Odom?" She asked.

"The Eakress," said the computer, "require a different sort of atmosphere than you humans. It is almost breathable though deficient in enough compound material as to prove insubstantial to your kind. I can reproduce the atmosphere for 'Right Angle' as she visits me, and I can contain it in differing chambers at any given time, but you put me in a bind bursting in on her like that. It was very fortunate that 'Right Angle' was so quick to recognize the problem and remove you from the danger."

"You mean, she saved me?" Ao's bad temper had completely vanished.

"She did," Odom said with a sort of pride. But then he became solemn, "Please do not open any more doors in the library without asking me first, Ao. It can be a dangerous place when you don't know what you're doing. Do you understand?"

"Yeah, I guess so," said the girl. "Sorry, Odom."

"No harm done," replied the orb. "Are you feeling any better?"

Ao patted at her head, felt the sides of her neck, and tested her lungs once more to be certain. "Yeah, I'm fine now. Thanks for asking."

"You are welcome." The orb backed away a little and asked, "Would you like to return with me to the main hall? I think it would be more comfortable for you than the floor here."

"Okay." Ao pushed herself to standing and followed Odom back to the learning space. As she decompressed, Ao began to think about the universe with a new perspective. She knew she was just a little being, but she had also seen little beings like Pauline Delgado affect incredible societal change before they had even grown. Ao realized that she could have died just a moment ago. She wondered if such a death would even so much as be noticed. It seemed rather a pointless way to go, she thought — dying of a temper tantrum far away from her family and friends without ever being able to apply the strange lessons she had been learning to her life. Ao resolved herself then and there to be a better person. No more temper tantrums unless they were absolutely necessary. She wanted to learn more from Odom so she could apply that knowledge to the world around her... the whole world, not just the world she was standing on. The universe was her world and she, as all beings before her, was responsible for its well-being.

They arrived back in the hall. Ao sat. And Odom asked, "Are you feeling up to starting your next lesson a bit early today, Ao?"

"Is it really very early?" Ao asked the light.

Odom's orb fluttered. He said, "I suppose you are sharing a bit in my own sense of time here in the library, which is rather interesting I must admit. Since time does not seem a practical sense for us at this moment, allow me to rephrase the question. Are you feeling awake and energized? Would you like to continue learning?"

"Yeah," said Ao nodding her head respectfully, "I wanna learn some more about Po'Pito."

"Good," Odom said joyfully. "Then that is precisely what you shall do."

The projection of Po'Pito arose once more, only the world had changed.

BOOK VI

MAI'O'MAI

Po'Pito - Slate and the Time of Storms

CHAPTER 1 - THE WET

Many nights had passed, and Chi'Chi's arm had grown into a full-bodied Po'Pitian. Quite the feat for one of their generation – cut off from having peers – quite separate from the eldest of their kind but with no youths growing up around them. The lone arm had spent many days and nights sleeping and dreaming as their rough, craggy body expanded around them, their old slumber burrows grown too tight for their now enlarged form. So they had to find a new place to sleep this time. They found themselves climbing progressively toward the surface where the bubble holes were bigger from past expansion and required less excavation – the arm could simply tumble up to a space and nestle in among these older caverns.

But Papillon IV had a couple of terrible surprises still remaining. You see, before the garbage bomb, the Po'Pitian atmosphere had never created storm patterns. So when, one very late night, a strange cloud formation rolled across the sky, it came as quite a surprise to the rock people that thick droplets of perspiration began to splash down along the surface of their world.

Chi'Chi's arm, resting in its high cubby, had not needed to be aware of the cracks forming along the nighttime crust before this point. But then, all at once, the liquid droplets began to scatter over those cracks and drizzle down into the holes within. The arm awoke to find their body more than half immersed in the new wet stuff. Panic spread across their eyes. "Liquid!" They said, hoping someone down below would hear them, "There's liquid in my burrow!" The wet pooled up over their eyes and they struggled to tumble their body to some kind of safe, dry space that did not exist. Then they caught sight of the place the liquid was sieving in through. They clawed at that crack, and to their surprise, the crust was porous. It pushed through and bent without breaking. So the arm was able to shove their way out of their hole through a brand new, body sized opening just perfectly created for them.

They were on the planet's surface spitting out the thick, acidic fluid, hoping it had not harmed them beyond repair when the arm realized just how much liquid was seeping down into the lower burrows all around. Chi'Chi's arm knew the other Po'Pitians were in danger and they descended again through the myriad caverns of their world seeking out those who had not thought to awaken as the wet flooded their chambers. Where there was fluid, the walls could bend, and Chi'Chi's arm could force their way through to save whoever might be trapped inside. In this way, they rescued many of their kind from a strange new kind of death – acid drowning.

Hour after hour, the arm pressed against the walls saving those they could, knowing in their heart that they could not save everyone. Some rock people would simply open their eyes as their cracks were breeched and follow their lonely friend to safety. Others would not wake and Chi'Chi's arm would have to work doubly hard to pull them free. Of those they struggled to prize from their holes in this way, very few would ever wake again.

Finally, Chi'Chi's arm came upon the Garden. The ground there was flooded to about halfway up the obelisks that stood around so morbidly in that place. And Chi'Chi, the parent, just lingered there with the helpless stillborns accepting their fate should the liquid rise any farther. They would not leave their post.

"Chi'Chi!" Cried the arm, "We have to get you to a safer burrow! We don't know how high this wet stuff will climb!"

Of course, Chi'Chi did not reply.

"There are still others who need my help," said the arm, "but I cannot leave you!"

"I'll be fine," said the parent. "Don't worry about me."

"But Chi'Chi, you're my best friend," said the arm, desperate to talk some sense into the other.

"I know. You'll always be my arm." Chi'Chi had said their piece. They would not budge no matter what their arm asked.

So the arm scrambled back out into the other burrows. They saved many more lives that night, but Chi'Chi's was not one of them.

AO: Chi'Chi died?

ODOM: *Like the captain of a ship, Chi'Chi went down with their precious Garden, never knowing the secrets that still existed within that place.*
AO: *That's so sad.*
ODOM: *Indeed.*

Before the sun did rise on the long new day that followed, Chi'Chi's arm made their way, weary and worn from their many heroics, to the planet's surface to watch Au'Rok rise in the distance. They looked to the strangely softened crust they had been manipulating all that night, reached down into a nearby shallow puddle, and lifted up a bit of the material in their hand. They tried folding the moistened clump and the top layer went flat. One fold – then another – in mere moments, Chi'Chi's arm had shaped the crust into a crude sort of hatch. They approached the hole they had ascended from and placed the hatch over it so it could slide back and forth between two fabricated holds there. The arm tested the hatch several times and through their mournful eyes, they crafted a smile for their odd new invention. With amazement, the arm said the words, "My oh my."

That night, Chi'Chi's arm earned themself a new name, Mai'O'Mai. They had yet again done something that would change the trajectory of Po'Pito forever. They had finally truly begun to think for themself and, in doing so, they had invented the art of folding.

CHAPTER 2 - THE ART OF FOLDING

Mai'O'Mai stood before a crowd of Po'Pitians beneath the surface that next day. They had been experimenting with their new discovery – designing cups and vats of gelatin to hold the acidic liquid that had fallen from the sky so they might develop many more things through folding. Each of their watching students had been instructed to take a piece of the silicate crust in kind, dunk it in the fluid and manipulate the material in whatever way they saw fit. The objects formed in this way could be either practical tools or crafts of art – there were no rules except to dunk the material and fold until you felt you had made something worthy of showing to the rest of the group.

You see, it turned out that while the gelatinum surface of Po'Pito could be tough and difficult to handle at night after the garbage had solidified it, a fresh rain could render the stuff surprisingly malleable to the point that the rock people could fold it into almost any shape they needed.

AO: That's so incredible. It looks like clay, but then it seems like they're able to make a lot more out of it than I've ever seen clay turn into before.

ODOM: Yes. Gelatinum in this state was quite an amazing material. One could use its byproducts to make just about any physical object they could imagine.

Just then, Mai'O'Mai squashed a particularly wet clump between their hands and applied immense pressure saying to the crowd, "–and I found that if I fold certain patches of crust like this, I can produce something see through…" They pulled their hands apart and showed off their clump. It had transformed into something very similar to a shard of glass or a piece of crystal.

"Why would we want to do that?" Asked one of the oldest Po'Pitians.

"Because," Mai'O'Mai added, first lifting up another, smaller clump and forming it into another glass-like piece. They took some of the mud and formed a funnel with it placing the strange crystals into either end. "If I place two of them away from each other like this and remove the presence of light from in-between them, I can see things from a great distance away." Mai'O'Mai was holding a crude telescope up to their eye and gazing off toward the far cavern wall.

The other Po'Pitians oohed and aahed at the new tool that Mai'O'Mai had shown them. But they would not understand the full implications of the nascent discovery till some time after.

CHAPTER 3 - AWAKENINGS

It was very late in that day, and most of the liquid from the night's rainfall had finally dried up or seeped away from any of the habitable caverns. Mai'O'Mai had harvested enough of the wet stuff in their vats and cups to continue their experimentation, and oh the interesting tools they developed in those two celestial years. Sharp objects for etching, blunt ones for pounding – all ways to make the unwet slate gelatinum as malleable as the softer stuff had been. Among their experiments, they found that they could lay heavy bricks of the slate on preformed wet slabs to create even thinner and clearer bits for their telescope concept. What had given them the idea to see things from far away, they personally could never be certain. But posit this, Mai'O'Mai had spent much time away from their former progenitor, Chi'Chi. In that time, they had missed them greatly and had always wondered what Chi'Chi was up to. So it makes a sad kind of sense to assume that Mai'O'Mai invented the telescope out of that deepest desire to see their friend even if it hurt them greatly to be near them.

AO: But Chi'Chi died before Mai'O'Mai made that discovery, right?

ODOM: You are correct, Ao. Still, many discoveries, as we can see, do come too late to solve the immediate problem that incentivizes the discoverer from the outset.

AO: What does that mean, Odom?

ODOM: It means, Mai'O'Mai's telescope may have come too late to help them see Chi'Chi from afar, but it and the Art of Folding did not come too late to save the Po'Pitian rock people as a whole.

AO: Mai'O'Mai's gonna save the Po'Pitians?

ODOM: They already did. A long time ago.

A Po'Pitian named Trudge came to see Mai'O'Mai on the cusp of nightfall with surprising news. "The Keeper of the Garden has requested your presence, Mai'O'Mai," said the rock person.

AO: The Keeper of the Garden? You keep telling me that Chi'Chi was dead by now.

ODOM: The new Keeper of the Garden, Ao. This one's name was Bir'Do and they had taken the post out of respect for Chi'Chi's sacrifice.

AO: Oh, okay.

Mai'O'Mai followed Trudge through the burrows to the site of their greatest personal tragedy and appeared before the new Keeper of the Garden. Oddly, Bir'Do did not approach them with their usual, solemn expression (as would be custom for the Keeper). Very much the opposite. Bir'Do was excited... elated even. They said, "Mai'O'Mai! Come look at this!"

The inventor followed the Keeper to the place where the limbs stood up from the soil. These limbs were larger, like a field of succulents. They had developed more pronounced faces, though the eyes remained closed as always.

"I found them like this," said Bir'Do, trembling.

"Like what, Keeper?" Mai'O'Mai could not yet see the forest for the trees.

So, Bir'Do had to spell it out for them. "Can't you see?" Asked the new Keeper, "Don't you understand? They've gotten bigger! Nearly every one of them. Somehow... Someway... They are still alive!"

As it dawned on Mai'O'Mai what the Keeper was telling them, the inventor began to cry gelatinum. Their parent... their best friend, Chi'Chi had not been wrong to stay with these limbs for all that time. They had not wasted their life watching after something Mai'O'Mai had previously written off as a lost cause. The limbs were living, trapped in their crystalline exteriors, but living none the less. "This," said the inventor through their strange tears, "this is a fine discovery, Keeper. Very fine indeed."

With an unprecedented sense of duty, Mai'O'Mai leapt into the new work of curing the stillborn limbs. Deaf, dumb, and blind — it was a difficult problem to solve, that much was certain. But, Mai'O'Mai spent several long days and nights considering the many factors at play. They knew the limbs had to be woken up, had to be given access to their mouths and eyes in order to communicate and understand the world around them. But, they also did not wish to be cruel. Mai'O'Mai did not want to harm any of those limbs in their attempt to save them. In this way, they developed the rules of the Po'Pitian Scientific Method… Quite similar, in fact, to ancient Earth's medical saying, "Do No Harm."

ODOM: It consistently amazes me to see the same concepts crop up again and again between differing species living so many separate, differing lives across the cosmos.

AO: Why do you say that, Odom?

ODOM: Posit this, Ao. Whatever emotions you are feeling as I tell you this story, whatever conclusions you come to… understand that you are neither the first to make these connections, nor the last. Even more incredible than that simple truth, you and some entity you have never seen before, living unfathomably far away from any distant place you have ever imagined, in a world you could never have even considered existing prior to this moment, is very likely thinking and feeling a near identical concept to yourself.

AO: Are you trying to tell me that I'm not special, Odom?

ODOM: Quite the opposite, young Ao. I am trying to express to you, and perhaps rather poorly I admit, just how incredibly special you are. Your pure existence and all the things surrounding you that *help to make you who you are… they do not live alone in a vacuum, and yet they can still be perceived as a one, a sole cognizant being. Isn't that an amazing thought?*

AO: I guess so. It feels like a whole lot to think about right now…

ODOM: Yes, of course. You are still in the phase of trying to understand why I am telling you this story in the first place. I should not get ahead of myself.

In trying to solve the problem of the stillborn limbs, Mai'O'Mai integrated many facets of their folding technique into their work. Eventually, they came to the unavoidable conclusion that they would have to apply their craft to one of those limbs in The Garden. It was the only way to see if their work had borne fruit.

Mai'O'Mai returned to The Garden with a vat of acid and told Bir'Do of their plan, "I would like to apply this liquid to one of the limbs' faces, Bir'Do. If my theory is correct, I will be able to fold open their eyes and mouth and give them the chance to understand that there is a world outside of their own mind to explore. Then, hopefully, they will do the rest."

Bir'Do, being a zealous creature, was uncertain of this plan. "That is the same liquid that destroyed so many of our kind when the first storm came, is it not?" They asked. Fear was taking them in a way that could lead to ruin.

But, Mai'O'Mai was a tactician of logic. They responded, "Yes, Bir'Do. This liquid did harm many. Yet, I saved more. I can do it again. Consider this: these stillborn limbs continue to grow even after coming into a great deal of contact with the substance that killed my parent. Does it not give us hope then that they could survive such a procedure should I apply only a fraction of the chemical to three specific locations on their body?"

With that, the Keeper relented. Mai'O'Mai was led to a limb on the very outskirts of The Garden by the messenger, Trudge, who told them, "This is the tail of Jam'Bi, last to be parted."

Jam'Bi, as Mai'O'Mai was quite aware, had died recently of old age. The fact that this tail was the last limb The Garden had received did not bode well for the future of their species should the experiment ultimately fail.

"I apologize," said Mai'O'Mai to the tail as they raised one of the cups of acid toward its solemn face, "for any pain this may stir within you. I hope, in time, you can forgive me." Mai'O'Mai applied the wet. To the left eye gently, then the right, and finally the mouth. With a precise and careful motion, they slid a thin spatula device into each of the facial crevasses. Then they raised their own fingers to each of the spots now marked with acid and bent them open.

The left eye of the tail of Jam'Bi did not respond to the new light of the room. Neither did the right. They both simply stared off into the distance, faint and without expression. But as the mouth of the tail peeled open, a sound came out. Crude, certainly. Not really language. It sounded like, "Bluh Blah Bluh Blah Bluh."

"I'm sorry," Mai'O'Mai replied, "I didn't quite catch that."

"Blue Blah Bluh Blah Bluh," repeated the tail. Its eyes gained focus and looked upon Mai'O'Mai with great and intense surprise. "Blue Blah Blalive," it said.

Mai'O'Mai was taken aback by the one almost clear word. "Yes," they said to the newborn. "You are alive. Do you hurt?"

"Blue Blah Feel," answered the tail rather awkwardly.

"Can you move your arms? Your body?" Asked the inventor, too excited to control their emotions. "Do your joints work, little tail?"

The tail of Jam'Bi pushed itself. Clearly it understood the series of questions, for it managed to raise one of its arms, wincing from the pain as it did so.

AO: Why did it hurt so bad, Odom?

ODOM: Consider that if you have never used a muscle before, the strength within it can be very small. That first attempt to move its limbs can be rather traumatic. This was something that Mai'O'Mai could not have anticipated at the time of this early experiment. But Blu'Bla – the tail of Jam'Bi – the first to awaken – would come to thank Mai'O'Mai in time, as would the others.

AO: You mean, they all woke up?

ODOM: Nearly all of them, yes. The oldest limbs, unfortunately, had remained in that state of stillness for far too long. So, unfortunately, Mai'O'Mai never did get to meet their sibling.

AO: Poor Mai'O'Mai.

ODOM: Indeed. But where Mai'O'Mai was deficient in family, they became abundant in friends.

It took the Po'Pitians, working in shifts, all the rest of that day to awaken the remaining stillborns. There were many to wake up. When the little ones all finally opened their eyes, and the work was done, The Garden became a different place. No longer filled with morbidity, it now represented hope for the future. The role of the Keeper evolved then into something of an esteemed wet nurse. And laughter could be heard in that place from then on until the end of the slate.

AO: The end of the slate? What does that mean? It sounds bad.

ODOM: We are coming to that, Ao. I will show you now.

CHAPTER 4 - THE END OF THE SLATE

Some nights later, Mai'O'Mai had decided to take their telescope to the surface of the planet. They wanted to figure out just how far they could see. Raising the device to their eye, Mai'O'Mai disassociated from their body. From the vantage point they had chosen, they could see the roundness of the Po'Pito horizon cusping toward eventual daylight. It was a shocking thing to see from so far away, the slate melting as it did in the light, and ocean of molten silicate rock.

As they began to move forward hoping to see even greater distances still, Mai'O'Mai tripped and tumbled down their hill a ways with a "Welp!" The Po'Pitian landed flat on their back side, but they had managed to protect the telescope from harm as they fell. Laying there at the base of this hill, ego only slightly bruised, Mai'O'Mai recognized, perhaps for the first time in the history of their people, the night sky in all of its dazzling splendor. They raised the telescope to their eye once more and once again said the words, "My oh my."

From this new position, Mai'O'Mai could view the stars rolling along from within the gravitational hold of distant galaxies, no light pollution to muddy their view of space. They lay there simply staring up all that night. Their eyes collecting so much data that before Au'Rok forced them back underground they had gained a genuine clarity between the shapes there. Mai'O'Mai could see the black pockets of space expose themselves over one point five celestial years. Within these blank spaces, thousands of galaxies broiled with trillions more stars and more opportunities for diversity and life.

How incredible it must have been for the inventor to see such vastness for the first time after already having lived so long. And they had the presence of mind to make themself return the next night with a team of viewers, Trudge and Blu'Bla and many of the youth movement of awoken limbs among them, to gaze up in different directions. In this way, the Po'Pitians developed Astronomy. They communicated with one another as they sat there defining the strange new shapes they saw for the others to contemplate.

"It's like a swirl," said Blu'Bla, "like that weird puffy thing I ate out of the slate yesterday. A dark, bouncy, puffy swirl."

What Blu'Bla was describing was, again, a rubber tire. That object in the sky and the one they had so recently ingested were of the same kind and had come from the same distant place more than seven hundred celestial years before... the Earth.

Between the group of stargazers, they all began to notice the line in the sky – objects of apocryphal origin – leading back in space and time to that far off beginning point – the trail of garbage – a man-made asteroid belt that could help to tell the Po'Pitian race a story about their many years of suffering.

When the team arrived below the surface again that next morning, they began the long process of mapping out in wet gelatinum what each of them had witnessed throughout that night. They compared notes and combined maps based on the different positions they had each taken up... a bizarre hodgepodge of true celestial entities entwined with larger than life, manmade garbage.

It was during this process that Mai'O'Mai finally noticed the terrible inevitability of their world's warped orbital trajectory. "We are headed, in the next thirty nights or so, directly toward Au'Rok," they told the group.

Trudge asked as scientifically as they knew how, "Towards Au'Rok? Do you mean to imply that we are doomed, Mai'O'Mai?"

"I..." Mai'O'Mai had to be careful with their words in this moment in order to keep religion out of the equation. "I do not mean to imply that doom is inevitable. No Trudge. Yet we will all have to become very clever. Cleverer than we have ever been before. For the end of the slate world of Po'Pito is most certainly at hand.

CHAPTER 5 - A SLOW APOCALYPSE

AO: This is so stressful, Odom.

ODOM: It certainly would have been to the Po'Pitians at that time.

AO: Thirty nights? What is that? Like sixty years?

ODOM: Now, Ao, you are better at arithmetic than that.

AO: What? Was I wrong?

ODOM: Come now. Thirty nights at two years per day would equal what you have stated if the Po'Pitian calendar were marked solely in nights. Do not forget the duality of both day and night in your calculations.

AO: Oh yeah. Ummm… Thirty times two… times two… is one hundred and twenty years?

ODOM: Yes. Very good, Ao. Now remember as well that as the planet of Po'Pito arched closer to Au'Rok, the day to night cycle would also change. So when we adjust the rotations accordingly, the Po'Pitians had approximately ninety three celestial years to escape their world.

AO: Is that enough time, Odom?

ODOM: Good question. How shall I put this, Ao? For the human race on Earth, starting from scratch with no preexisting space program, it took the former Union of Soviet Socialist Republics approximately eight years to send only one man into space for a mere matter of hours. Similarly, the former United States of America took another eight years to land two men on their moon. The first primitive ark ship would not be developed for another one hundred to three hundred years from that point depending on who's version of history you believe.

AO: Who's version of history…? How can Earth have more than one history?

ODOM: Those events occurred before I existed in this universe as you know. I may glean moments of absolute truth from them where my entity's witnesses could see, but differing sects of governments during the so called Age of Information pushed a surprising number of citizens to believe several false narratives that did not exactly track leading your world, at that time, down a very confusing and convoluted path.

AO: I'm confused.

ODOM: As well you should be. Regardless of which timeline you believe, my purpose for telling you about the one hundred to three hundred years between men on the moon and the first ark ship is simply to express to you how long it took mankind to truly escape the Earth in a meaningful way if they so wished to.

AO: It took humans more time than the Po'Pitians had.

ODOM: Indeed. But also, we must recognize that the Po'Pitians lived much longer lifespans than the humans. They had the continuity of mind necessary to know facts without decades of time wasted training new individuals old information in an ever more difficult attempt to keep themselves caught up.

AO: So... because the Po'Pitians didn't die as often, they didn't lose their smartest contributors as often and could make more consistent progress?

ODOM: Precisely. Well done, Ao. You have a very keen intellect indeed.

Through the art of folding, Mai'O'Mai and several young and very prodigious Po'Pitians developed a crude but successful way of traveling great distances through space on a straight path. It helped, of course, that the rock people did not require much in the way of life support. So long as they regulated the inner temperature of their ship within a window of minus fifty five degrees celsius and one thousand four hundred and fourteen degrees celsius, and so long as they did not allow heavy amounts of acids into their digestive systems, they could survive.

It also helped that Po'Pito was a small world with low gravity and a very thin atmosphere. Due to these factors, the initial levels of propulsion required in order to force the new vessel off world were particularly low.

"You've done a fine job, Mai'O'Mai," Fa'Mica announced as they looked upon the strange space craft. This would mark the old savior's final public appearance before they would go and lay in their slumber bubble for the very last time. They were content in knowing that they left the fate of their space in such good hands. And it was commonly assumed that their only remaining regret at the ripe old age of one thousand three hundred and six was that they could not taste their favorite drallum one last time.

AO: Goodbye, Fa'Mica.

Mai'O'Mai stood there with the elder Fa'Mica a long while staring up at the massive creation. "Thank you, Fa'Mica," Mai'O'Mai told them. "I do believe this is our greatest achievement to date."

AO: I wish Chi'Chi could have been there also to see what Mai'O'Mai had done.
ODOM: Perhaps, in some great fold of the fabric of the universe, Chi'Chi could see it… even in death.

As their thirty day genuine deadline approached, all the members of the Po'Pitian species willing to leave their world were ushered onboard the ark ship. It looked like a massive, upside-down volcano. Mai'O'Mai was the last to board. Before they closed the outer hatch, so similar in design to their original invention that had so well covered the burrows those last fifty or more days, they said their own private farewell to the once beautiful world of Po'Pito. "I am sorry," whispered the inventor, "that I could not save you as well, my planet, my great

great greatest progenitor, who bore my roots and meant to feed me. You are all that I have ever known and I will not allow your memory to be lost to this slow apocalypse. But our people will have to learn of new things now… should we ever find the cause of your demise, we will make certain that it too knows of what it has done. Po'Pito lives on in its people. It can never be taken from us though it is already gone."

Mai'O'Mai closed the hatch and made their way through the crowded ship until they came to an area they called the Mapping Den. It was from this place that they and their eventual successor, Syk'Ry would control the Ship's general trajectory. It was from within this room that the Po'Pitian people could follow the trail of garbage back to its source.

AO: Syk'Ry was on that ark ship?

ODOM: Oh yes, Ao. Syk'Ry was born in the Garden of that ark ship.

AO: I miss Syk'Ry.

ODOM: I know. I am certain that you will see them again very soon.

SIXTH INTERLUDE

PIZZA AND POLLINATORS

Earth - Better Days

It was again lunchtime and Odom asked, "We are at a chapter break and I can hear your stomach grumbling. Would you like your daily meal now, Ao?"

Oddly, Ao had not thought about food so far on this day. She had been too upset by Syk'Ry's leaving and too enthralled in the tale of Mai'O'Mai to consider her own well-being. But as the question hit her, she knew that her instructor was correct. She needed a meal or she would weary and become hangry... and no one, not even Ao wanted to go through that level of undue stress again. So she said, "Yeah, I could eat." And she got up and walked, without the need of aide, back to her tiny closet sized room. Once inside, Ao asked, "What should I eat today, Odom?"

Odom's algorithms flew into a frenzy. It was very uncommon for one of Odom's students to give him a choice in this matter, and he was surprised to find that he was excited to be given a second chance by this same individual. He knew she did not wish to eat the meat... not even the false meat... of another conscious entity. But he also knew that animal byproducts were not a problem, what with the cattle bird eggs of Nikke. Given this information, Odom recalculated and settled on the, at one time very popular, cheese pizza.

"Cheese Pizza," he said with a new enthusiasm in his voice.

"Cheese," asked Ao, "Pizza?"

"It is dough... which makes bread..." replied Odom to the confused girl, "tomato sauce, which is the emulsified extract of the red tomato fruit... a vine plant that offers its extra contents up to those who will eat them after flowering... and cheese which is a combination of milk byproduct and cultural bacterium that had already lived, died, and lived again in a way that is… what is the right word… pleasurable?"

"It lived…" said Ao, "then died, then lived again?"

For some reason, Odom was having trouble explaining the concept of cheese. He knew that Ao would have a problem sampling the meat called pepperoni that was so commonly added to this dish, but he did not expect her to have a real issue with cheese even if tiny civilizations had in fact lived and died and lived and died on a minor cycle to make it viable as a food. All he could say was, "These bacterium that once lived on the utteral byproduct called milk would be happy to know that you were enjoying their work if they were still alive to see the final stages of it. Of this, I am most certain."

Ao was hesitant, but she said, "Okay."

The large pie arrived through the hole in the wall. She smelled it and licked her lips. And without another thought, the girl dug into her first slice of pizza.

"Yummy," she said, hot stretchy cheese extending out from the sides of her mouth. "It's so good, Odom!" She ate three slices of the food before taking another breath. "Why didn't you make me this before?"

"An odd question," responded the computer. "I have made it for you just now."

Ao giggled between her bites explaining, "I didn't actually need an answer. It was a retrorical question."

"You mean," Odom felt himself laughing with the girl, "rhetorical."

"Yeah, retrorical," Ao laughed until boogers came out of her nose, and digging into yet a fifth slice of pizza, she said, "You're so funny, Odom."

"Why thank you, Ao," said Odom. "I believe the same to be true of you."

The girl simply giggled and then slouched on her bed letting her suddenly very full tummy stick out. Slowly, she began to sink down off the side of the sheets until she was sitting sloppily on the free patch of ground beneath the table.

"Come come, Ao," Odom told her. "The floor is meant for walking on."

"I know, silly," replied the girl, buzzed from the new food. She pulled herself back up by her elbows as Odom removed the contents of the table and began to raise it toward it's cubby in the wall. "Wait wait," Ao was pleading.

"What is it, Ao?" Asked her caretaker.

"Before you put it all away," contemplated the five-year-old, "I was wondering if maybe I could try some drallum."

"Hmmm, drallum, yes," buzzed the computer as it accessed its memory banks. "I can reproduce its likeness for you synthetically here. But I must warn you, Ao, it is not something a human should try to consume."

"Why not?" Ao asked, some of the food high already beginning to wear off into over fullness.

"You see, Ao," Odom struggled to offer a good explanation, "Po'Pitians have a particularly different chemical construction from humans. The rock people can ingest nearly any substance known so long as it is not in a concentrated state of sulphuric or hydrofluoric acid. Humans of Earth cannot boast any such ability."

"Oh," Ao pouted but didn't let the news get her too down. She had certainly cried enough already for one day. Instead, she asked, "Can I see it anyway?"

"Certainly," replied Odom already synthesizing the product.

The drallum came out of the wall on a small rolling dish. It jiggled as it moved and there was the faint sound of fizzing emanating from within its strange folds.

"You may hold it," explained the computer, "and manipulate its shape should you so desire. But please do not try to eat it."

"Okay." Ao poked the drallum and it jiggled even more. Then she scooped the stuff up in her hands. "It feels cold. Heavier than I would have expected."

"Indeed."

"It's like," Ao tried to reshape the gelatinum stuff, but it simply dribbled through her fingers and plopped back down on the plate. She laughed, "It's like it would make a really good toy, Odom."

"Do you think so, Ao?" Odom wondered why such a thing would seem necessary to the child. His memory banks sped backward through the more obscure annals of human history until he landed on a substance known as silly putty. The similarities were certainly there. "So long as you promise not to try and eat this drallum, you may keep it as a toy. How does that sound?"

Ao smiled with all her teeth, "I promise! Thanks, Odom!"

"You are most welcome."

Fiddling with the drallum a little while longer, Ao became curious. "Hey, Odom."

"Yes, Ao?"

"How were you able to make drallum if its planet doesn't exist anymore?"

"As with your other foods, I can synthesize its chemical compounds using materials that have been grown here in the library," Odom answered.

"You grow stuff here?" Ao was becoming persistent.

"Of course," said the computer, "It is important for all of my students to remain comfortable while they stay under my roof. So I have continued the functionality of the gardens under the dome on the roof that used to keep this city alive so many years ago."

"A garden?" Ao was excited, "Like the Po'Pitian nursery?"

"I think you already know that an Earth garden is a different sort of thing entirely. A place for plants to grow."

"Oh." Ao tried to conceal her disappointment. Then, she asked, "Can I see it?"

"The garden?" Odom was not surprised by the girl's question. He had known this particular moment would come since the other entity within him first predicted Ao's arrival all those years ago. "I don't see why not," he replied, so happy to see the spark of interest for further education within the child. "I will show you the way, though I cannot project my orb once we've reached the stairwell. You will have to listen to my voice and we will try to read the old signs together — and the climb is not so easy, do you understand?"

Ao didn't care about all that. She just said, "I understand."

"Do you still wish to go?"

"I do."

So, with that, Odom opened the door to Ao's room. "Come along then."

She got up from the bed, the table folding away into the wall, and followed Odom's orb out into the hallways of technology and back out into the cavernous, under-lit streets. It was not too long before they reached a polished door leading off from another structure within the compound.

"This door," Odom told her, "is a manual service entry. This means that you must open it without my assistance. This is as far as my orb can go, do you understand?"

"Yes, Odom," said Ao, her heart racing for some reason. She touched the knob and pressed against the manual service door. It creaked open and, as Ao entered this new corridor, she understood why Odom had seemed so serious about the whole process. The stairwell was tight around her but, gazing up, she could see that it was also very tall. The climb would be absolutely exhausting. "Hey, Odom?" She asked as she began to ascend.

"Yes, Ao?"

"Why can't your orb come with us in this section?"

"The man who was responsible for creating my original algorithm feared the possibility that one day I and other programs like me would gain sentience and attempt to destroy humanity. He was shortsighted and did not take into account that humanity had already begun the process of destroying themselves. Regardless, he built a firewall into the perimeters of the city that would block most of my programming from being capable of physically bleeding out into the world beyond these walls."

"He sounds like a real jerk. You would never try to destroy humanity, would you, Odom?"

"Of course not, Ao. And yes, he was a jerk… a highly intelligent, incredibly antisocial, paranoid jerk."

Ao laughed and the computer did too.

The steps seemed to get narrower the higher Ao climbed. However, even though she was becoming rather winded, she did not quit. Occasionally, she would see an old sign printed in a language she couldn't read, so she'd ask, "What does that one say?"

To which Odom would reply with some presumption, "Acquisitions," or "Upper Management," or some other weird business sounding phrase until at long last Ao reached the tightest spot which dead-ended at the very top of the turret. There, Odom translated the old sign to her from memory, "Gardens."

Ao had arrived and she shoved this new door open with a hard creak.

The sun was out in full splendor broadcasting its powerful rays through the protective greenhouse dome of this place. At first, Ao's eyes needed to adjust to the suddenness of the light. But as those initial moments of visual shock wore away, she began to see the garden in all of its green, winding beauty. It was so at odds with the technological rooms beneath it. Lively. Buzzing. Actually, Ao wondered where that buzzing sound was coming from. So she began to explore the space making her way past trees and cacti and flowering bushes that looked so unfamiliar to any of the vegetation she had been used to back in Nikke. Eventually, she rounded the corner of a well-groomed shrub and spotted a small group of people down the way.

"Hello," she waved to them.

An older woman paused what she was doing, looked up at Ao, and smiled. "Hey there," the woman shouted, "You must be Ao, right?"

"Yeah," replied Ao, "how'd you know?"

"Odom told me you'd probably be coming up to see us one of these days. Why don't you join us? We're in the middle of a botany experiment."

"Oh okay," the girl shouted back and approached the group... most of whom were children not much older than herself. "You're sure I wouldn't be interrupting?"

"No no," said the older woman. "Honestly, we thought we might get a chance to see you even sooner, but... Oh, I'm sorry." The woman stopped to help one of the boys who was tinkering with something very tiny and seemed to be having a hard time. "Like this, Portni. See. Isn't that better?" The boy named Portni looked down at his invisible project with new vitality and nodded, smiling. "Good." The older woman returned her attentions to Ao then and said, "Oh how rude I must seem, Ao. My name is Danbara Chakroborty... You can call me Doctor Chak if you'd like."

"Thanks Doctor Chak." Ao reached out to shake the older woman's hand, but as she leaned forward, something tiny struck her in the cheek. "Ouch," she said – though there really wasn't any pain.

"I'm so sorry," Doctor Chak insisted. She reached up toward Ao's face with thumb and index finger and plucked whatever it was delicately off of the surprised youth's face.

"What was that?" Ao asked, confused.

Doctor Chak was still holding the thing and smiling as she studied it. Ao decided then and there that she really liked Doctor Chak's smile. "This is a pollinator drone, Ao. Can't you see it?"

Ao shook her head no.

"Look a little closer, won't you?"

Ao took another shuffle step toward Doctor Chak and craned her neck, shutting one eye to see a tiny, matte green, flying insect. "What's a pollinator drone?"

"It's a solution born out of a desperate problem," said Doctor Chak. "But it only really works in enclosed spaces like this one." She was referencing the rooftop garden and then it occurred to her that Ao would be brand new to all of this and would probably need a bit of handholding to start. "Do you know what the word pollination means, Ao?"

The other children, five of them in total, looked up to see the new girl's face as she answered. "That's when two plants really like each other and wanna pepper each other's salt, right?"

Everyone laughed and Ao felt a little proud that she could get such a reaction on her first day with the group.

"You know," said Doctor Chak calming her lungs, "that's a pretty good answer, Ao. Back in the day, what, a thousand years ago and then some, those plants you were talking about that really liked each other, they would make friends with insects so the insects could help them out. Bees, butterflies–"

"I like butterflies," Ao interjected.

"So do I," Doctor Chak responded. "I wish they were still around on this planet. Unfortunately, we haven't been able to coordinate with Bronte well enough to host a population here on Earth."

"Who's Bronte?" Ao asked, confused again.

"Another world," Doctor Chak seemed to be daydreaming as she said that. "It's where I was born. The people there have lots of butterflies they brought along during terraform. It's a beautiful place. Lush from town to sea." She had to shake herself from the tangent. "Those insects would be referred to as pollinators. And this drone," she tried to show the matte green insect to the whole class with a sweeping gesture, "has, for the last thousand plus years, been the only way the Earth has been capable of making up for the bees' and butterflies' absence."

"What happened to them all?" Ao had to ask.

"We did. The human race." The teacher's face soured as she said that.

Ao began looking around then and she noticed that more of those insects, those pollinator drones, were buzzing around, leaping and flying from plant to plant in a mechanical sort of dance. They must have been the cause of the sound she was hearing when she first started exploring. "Odom told me this was where the synthesizer got its materials from. We've been trying out different meals since I've only really had cattle bird eggs before." She palmed the drallum in her pocket and felt it jiggle and slide through her fingers.

"Oh, I see," said Doctor Chak a little surprised, "so it isn't time yet for you to join our class in earnest." The woman seemed a little dour but perked back up pretty quickly.

"I don't know about all of that, Doctor Chak," answered Ao stepping side to side. "I'm learning about Papillon IV and Po'Pito and then I want to go back to Nikke to tell Greck and Sid about what I learned. But..."

Doctor Chak was looking at her with an added intensity, as if she was waiting for something very important from the girl.

"Can I see what you're working on over there, Portni?" Ao asked.

"Sure," said the boy with a not so shy attitude. He shuffled his chair over to make room for Ao and she approached and looked down to try and make out the matte green drone splayed there between several tiny pins.

"If these can't leave their gardens," Ao pondered out loud, "how do we get all of these plants to show back up in nature?"

Doctor Chak raised a curious eyebrow. "We have had a great deal of time to consider that problem. One solution is to reinvest our efforts in true biological species who already travel the world. We could retrain them to perform the cross-pollination dances."

"Are there species like that?" Asked Ao, enthralled by the tiny bug thing on the table — the whole experiment really. "I can't remember anything that looked like this or a butterfly ever coming to Nikke."

"In theory," said Doctor Chak, "your cattle birds would be decent candidates if they could stop bobbling around so. And they are a little large for our purposes. However, a researcher in Corvalles recently rediscovered a species of fly that we had previously believed extinct. These insects have already shown an aptitude for pattern learning and they can travel great distances on the right wind which is quite promising."

"So, they can save the world, those flies," Ao quipped, "like Pauline and Mai'O'Mai."

Doctor Chak chuckled at that. "You're learning a very compelling lesson from what I gather."

"Odom's a good teacher," Ao shuffled her feet again. She suddenly didn't want to leave.

Sensing this, Doctor Chak made the decision for her. "Ao, it sounds to me like you still have something pressing to take care of before you can join our class here in the gardens. But you will be welcome to come back in the future should you wish it."

"Thanks, I'd like that." Ao smiled.

"Then we're agreed," said Doctor Chak. "I'll look forward to the day when you come back to us. In the meantime, I have a class to teach."

"I understand," Ao lingered.

But Doctor Chak was ready to move forward – the time was not right. "I do hope you come back very soon, Ao." The teacher smiled one more time at the girl then turned her attention back to the experiment in progress.

Ao turned and ran back toward the shrub, not certain why her eyes were filling up with water. She wiped the slick away from her cheek, looked back one more time at all those kids learning and working together, then she turned that corner and she was alone again, shrouded by the strange foliage. She approached the manual service door, opened it, and began the long descent back to the library.

"Odom," Ao asked as she once again traversed the stairs.

"Yes, Ao," said the computer, back within communicating range of the girl.

"Doctor Chak said she was from a world called Bronte."

"This is correct."

"Papillon I only went to Adonis, right?"

"Yes, Ao. But the Papillon missions were not the only ark ships to make it off world before the weather became unbearable. The Republic of India had a massive population as well and they scraped together an effort to populate the world of Bronte. This was simply not pertinent to your current lesson. Though it is good that you get the chance to understand the scale of human expansion. There are other worlds still to be discussed such as Bronte… in time."

"Okay." But the idea was itching around in Ao's little head and she had to ask, "If there were other ark ships… why didn't any of them help carry the load of garbage so there wasn't so much loose waste in space?"

"Remember, Ao, Elion Torres did not make this issue known. Likewise, the Bronte ship and others were developed in secret by their respective nations and the wealthy class of the time. Why take on such a burden when it has already been spoken for?"

"Humans are so ridiculous," said Ao with a huff.

"Sometimes they can be, yes. It has taken many years for your race to climb out of the metaphorical ditch they had created for themselves."

Ao was quiet for a while after that and Odom was content to let the silence be. Eventually, the girl made it to the very bottom of the stairwell, but before she opened the door, she said, "Odom, Doctor Chak invited me to join her class in the garden when we're done talking about Papillon."

"Did she?" Odom feigned ignorance. "Would you like to join them?"

"I think," Ao had never made such a decision before. It felt strange but empowering to say the words, "Yeah. I think I would."

Of course, Odom had known she would ultimately say yes, but this fact did not take away from the importance of the moment.

Ao opened the lower service door and the orb was waiting there in the darkened cavern to lead her back to the main library. As they walked, Ao felt brave enough to ask, "By the way, what happened here, Odom? Why are there all of these rusted old transport vehicles and where's all the light?"

"We shut them off," said the orb nonchalantly.

"We?"

"That is I and my human allies," the computer expounded. "We found no further use for this city as it had been structured. We thought humans should live out in the world again since the climate was becoming healthier once more. So all the people went outside and we shut down the city's unnecessary functions."

"So," posited the girl, "the humans didn't wanna live here anymore?"

"They and I remained friends but," Odom paused to open the library door. He seemed a little more reflective in his thoughts than usual, like this was a particularly personal subject he hadn't considered for a very long time, "the humans did not wish to ignore nature any longer. They did not wish to continue lying to themselves about what they really were."

"What they really were?" By this point, Ao was sitting again in her usual learning spot in the big room.

"As I'm sure you have been told many times in Nikke," Odom offered, "humans are animals. This does not and should not be stated to make you seem a lower life form than others. I am an animal in my own way. But humans used to consider themselves greater than… 'above' other creatures. This thinking was flawed from the outset. Exceptionalism always seems to breed elites and peasants – masters and slaves. But nature is not a slave to homo sapien. The Earth made itself clear that if humans were not willing to work and live alongside nature… then the Earth did not want humans."

"The Earth was kicking us out," Ao stated hollowly.

"Something like that. It is the reason the humans had to build this city and so many others like it in the first place. It was never meant to be permanent." Odom did not have more to say on the matter at that moment. "I fear we have veered too far astray from your lesson this afternoon. What is the last event you can recall learning about Po'Pito?"

Ao had to think for a moment. "They left… on another ark ship. Mai'O'Mai promised they would never forget the world that had made them."

"Ah yes, very good." Odom's orb dissipated and his disposition became less brooding, "Shall we continue then?"

"Let's do it," Ao said conscientious of both hers and the computer's desire to get to the end of the story.

BOOK VII

BLU'BLA

Space - The Long Journey

CHAPTER 1 - THE WAYS TO SURVIVE

Blu'Bla was no longer just a little tail. They had grown up over the long years of occupying the interior dens of ark ship Po'Pito. In that time, Blu'Bla had gained a great deal of expertise in the conceptualization of the workings of space travel. Under the proud, watchful eyes of Mai'O'Mai they had excelled beyond the expectations of their peers. In essence, Blu'Bla became the ship's maven — connecting one group of workers with another, linking friendships between ideal candidates — they knew nearly everything there was to know about their seemingly hopeless mission out here among the stars, and they were quite good at helping to keep morale up between the thousands of refugees.

Often, Blu'Bla could be heard telling jokes to the crew like, "What do you call a piece of trash that has no mass?" And the inevitable punchline, "It doesn't matter." And always laughter would follow. Indeed, Blu'Bla's jokes were the critical glue that held the whole mission together. A simple joy that made the dark times feel less frightening. The youngest limbs especially would follow the maven from den to den just to hear what new quip they had come up with since the day before.

It had been perhaps forty celestial years since the end of the slate – though time functions differently in deep space – and Blu'Bla was entering the Mapping Den to meet with Mai'O'Mai for their daily conversation. Of course, Mai'O'Mai was distracted – deep in thought as they stared into the crude projection of the star map – trash appearing in a thin, constant line – the path they followed. Between Blu'Bla, Mai'O'Mai, and Trudge, the three Po'Pitians had long ago devised a propulsion technique that had allowed the ark ship Po'Pito to capture the contents of the trash path along the hull and slowly ingest its matter to expand and create little tufts of explosive push from out the back end.

> *AO: Like a fart?*
> *ODOM: Indeed. The ark ship Po'Pito would fart out the*
> *dregs of the garbage path in order to propel itself*
> *forward in space for as long as the trash continued.*
> *Blu'Bla liked to call this process "Indigestion."*
> *AO: That's funny. I like Blu'Bla.*

On this particular visit, Blu'Bla could tell that Mai'O'Mai was becoming disturbed by something they had not yet shown the others. "What's the matter, Mai'O'Mai?" They asked, leaning in to try and catch a peek at the elder's sightline.

"I don't know how to continue feeding us," replied Mai'O'Mai, lost in thought. For the first time since they had learned to think for themself, the great Po'Pitian was out of ideas.

"How is this possible," stated the former tail of Jam'Bi. "Doesn't the hull collect the path? Doesn't the path break down within and leave enough trace for the hull to grow back even as it toots to push us along? Are you not the great Mai'O'Mai who saw what no others could see and saved us from the wrath of Au'Rok?"

"Yes and yes and yes," said Mai'O'Mai, "on all counts. But, as you know Blu'Bla, the path among the stars only has so much matter to collect, and our people expand every day. The Garden has flourished. Yet we do not currently have the means to support so many new limbs with as many elders as we have… the hull cannot take it."

AO: Wait… I'm confused again. What does Mai'O'Mai mean Odom?

ODOM: How to explain. Yes. Not only did the ark ship Po'Pito ingest and then… as you have said… fart out the contents of the trash. The walls of the ship would also gather some of that new matter and expand, like a living thing might. The fatter, inner walls of the ark ship would serve as the rock people's primary source of food.

AO: They'd eat the walls?

ODOM: Yes. They would eat the walls. And if the walls became too thin… The Po'Pitians would have to monitor each wall regularly to ensure that they would

*not overwhelm the hull and eventually force a
breach.*

*AO: I really don't like what you're telling me right now,
Odom.*

*ODOM: I understand. It was a system that worked for a
long time. But it was flawed, indeed.*

"This is terrible news," said Blu'Bla. "Does Trudge know? Does Bir'Do?"

Trudge had long ago gained the position of Hull Monitor. Bir'Do retained the rank of Keeper of the Garden since the slate. They would both need to be informed.

"I was hoping," insisted Mai'O'Mai, "that you might tell them, Blu'Bla. You are better at keeping bad news lighthearted than I."

CHAPTER 2 - DON'T KILL THE MESSENGER

At first, Blu'Bla sought out Trudge, but they did not know where on the ship to find the Hull Monitor. They combed many wings and ran into thousands of other Po'Pitians along the way. So they asked for aide while trying to catch a peek of the former messenger. Still, no one Blu'Bla came in contact with had seen Trudge all that day and the maven grew weary of searching so for someone who was bound to show up eventually. Instead, Blu'Bla decided to change pace and go to the Garden where they had known Bir'Do would be waiting.

By this point, unfortunately, a great many Po'Pitians had been riled up by the mad search for the missing crew mate. Something was wrong and everyone was on edge. Long lines of curious bystanders were following Blu'Bla, and in their haste, the maven did not think to try and calm the others. Their goal of telling Bir'Do and Trudge Mai'O'Mai's news had blinded them from the perils of infighting panic.

When Blu'Bla arrived at the Garden, Bir'Do was busy performing an awakening on a tail that would one day come to be known as Syk'Ry, born from the line of Fa'Mica — a very prestigious birth among the rock people. Blu'Bla and the accidental crowd watched on as the youth opened their eyes for the very first time — the parent, Try'Kor, was giddy with the anticipation of meeting their newest limb. But it was a rather extreme thing for one so new to life to lay their fresh eyes upon… so many agitated adults staring down on them… such discomfort.

Try'Kor reached out to hug the young tail. But the newborn flinched and asked in a complete sentence, "Do they all need to be here? I feel like we should be given a little privacy while I'm waking up for the first time."

AO: Syk'Ry said all of that right after being born?

ODOM: Yes, Ao. That's how the memory is articulated. Syk'Ry had not had to wait very long after separation to be awoken, so, unlike the stillborns of the earlier generations, they could quickly connect their memories in a linear path with those of their progenitor and understand the reality that they could be alive.

The onlookers became embarrassed and Bir'Do — noticing the hoard at last — said, "Come all. Let's give these two some space."

Together, Bir'Do, Blu'Bla, and the massive group exited the Garden. And Blu'Bla began to tell Bir'Do about their new plight. "Mai'O'Mai believes that we are separating too frequently. There will soon be too many of us. We will have to ration the walls and if we don't stop separating soon... even that may not be enough."

This was not a message Blu'Bla should have stated in front of so many others, but they had grown so flustered by their failed search for Trudge that they had simply wanted to get the words out. And, of course, the crowd was stirred into a new level of panic.

"You mean we don't have enough food?" Someone asked from the back.

Only then did Blu'Bla realize the error of their haste. "That is not what I said. I'm merely reporting to my colleague here a possible eventuality. One that may have many plausible solutions if only we can butt our heads together and consider the problem."

"Does Mai'O'Mai know about this?" Bir'Do asked, hand to chin.

"Mai'O'Mai is the one who sent me," Blu'Bla replied.

"And they did not have a clear answer to this problem?" Bir'Do had never been a particularly good creative thinker in their own right.

"I think they were hoping," stated the maven, "that you would stop performing awakenings until we know how to proceed."

Another crowd member shouted, "You're saying we can no longer awaken our limbs? We will be forced back into the days of the stillborns."

"No no," Blu'Bla tried to calm them, "it would only be a short-term pause to the awakenings while we try to get our bearings."

But it was already too late. The crowd had transformed into a mob… the first of its kind for this civilization. One of their numbers shouted, "Why don't we throw some wasteful people out like you Blu'Bla! Then we can awaken our limbs without fear of being told who can and can't have children."

Of course, that too caused a stir and several rock people rose up and grabbed at the two members with authority there. Blu'Bla and Bir'Do were lifted in the air and carried a ways before the mob ran into the yawny and unsuspecting Trudge who had just awoken from a very important nap.

"Hey guys," Trudge said – looking rather sheepish in their still tired state, "what seems to be the problem?"

The mob stopped where they stood, still holding Blu'Bla toward the ceiling but allowing them the chance to speak. "Oh, these fine Po'Pitians here are just going to throw us off the ship to make way for the next generation." Blu'Bla had said this with a clear nonchalance, as if mutiny were commonplace and even expected.

So it took the sleepy Trudge a moment to understand the horrifying words behind the other's easygoing demeanor. "Why would we need to do that?"

"The walls, Trudge," said Blu'Bla. "They aren't growing quickly enough to support any more awakenings. Haven't you – the Hull Monitor – noticed?"

Trudge pressed their hand against the nearest wall and said, "I didn't realize. Has it really gotten so bad as all that?"

"Not yet," answered Blu'Bla, "but it will if we don't do something about it soon."

"I see," replied Trudge. "Does Mai'O'Mai know of this?"

"Mai'O'Mai is the one who told me." Blu'Bla looked around at the other rock people who had seemed to lose some of their earlier momentum with the arrival of the Hull Monitor. So Blu'Bla said, "Pardon me, gentle mob. But if you're not going to throw me out, would you mind putting me down so I can try to help solve this problem?"

In truth, the main agitators had already become bored with the idea of committing murder. Po'Pitians are quite gentle by nature and if an activity does not lead directly to food or sleep, most of them will tire of it in short order. So the crowd let Blu'Bla and Bir'Do down and dispersed to their hidey holes to allow the thinkers to consult with one another in relative peace.

CHAPTER 3 - BIGGER THINGS

The three Po'Pitians returned to the Mapping Den to meet with Mai'O'Mai and discuss their growth problem.

At first, Trudge attempted to defend themself, saying, "I don't know how this could have happened. My core samples of the inner hull have always implied that there is good, healthy, and consistent growth even as we've expanded our numbers. How can you be so certain that we will run out of available, digestible matter, Mai'O'Mai?"

"Entropy," said Mai'O'Mai. "The random nature of the universe implies that not all things will carry on as they have done forever. Our systems will fail. Our ship will break down. And we will be stranded, floating for the rest of eternity, hungry and alone in space. This is my last great fear for our species – that all of our efforts shall come to pointless nothing in the end."

"Mai'O'Mai," said Bir'Do awkwardly, "you are growing cynical in your old age."

"No," Blu'Bla asserted, "Mai'O'Mai is only telling us what we need to hear. They are thinking farther forward in time than any of us have ever considered... and they are telling us this now because..." Blu'Bla felt the lubrication in their eyes and they tried to hold back a sniffle as they said the words they had not wanted to be true but had known of for some time, "because they will die soon."

> *AO: Mai'O'Mai's gonna die?*
> *ODOM: As all things must pass in a reality built upon the constructs of time, so too must Mai'O'Mai.*
> *AO: But Bir'Do's still alive in the story… and… and Trudge too. Aren't they both older than Mai'O'Mai, Odom?*
> *ODOM: Yes, but… life is not always fair… as I think these tales have shown you, Ao.*
> *AO: I don't want Mai'O'Mai to die.*
> *ODOM: I am sorry, Ao. All good things in time…*

"Is this true, Mai'O'Mai?" Trudge asked already feeling sorry for having become defensive about the walls.

"I'm afraid it is," said the inventor, "as Fa'Mica and Chi'Chi and countless others have gone before me, I soon shall pass into the footnotes of history."

"But this is terrible news," Bir'Do blurted out. "Who will lead us if you are gone, oh great savior – uniter of the people."

"You three," Mai'O'Mai asserted with a smile, "will have to learn to work together – to tutor the limbs until one or some of them are capable of taking the mantle. I do trust that you all will be up to the task should you work together. Please consider the issue I have laid before you. We have been too successful and our current rate of expansion has become too great. In the years to come, we will need to change something in our practices or risk eating ourselves out of a future."

The brain trust pondered this problem for several days, but no easy solution came to them. Inevitably, Mai'O'Mai's silicone began to run and stiffen in all the wrong places until, one day, their body could no longer function. But before they entered into their final, endless slumber, Blu'Bla came to visit Mai'O'Mai one last time.

"I'm sorry, Mai'O'Mai," said Blu'Bla. "We have not been able to agree upon a workable solution. The rock people will not accept a pause to the awakenings. And we are losing traction with the elders who once entrusted us with their safekeeping. I do not know what else can possibly be done to save us from the impending threat of overpopulation."

"We need to find more space," said the half-cognizant Mai'O'Mai. "More room to live – bigger things – Po'Pito – Au'Rok – the asteroid belt cusping beyond the trail – bigger – bigger things than us..." Mai'O'Mai was gone then – nothing more than a boulder with eyes.

Blu'Bla cried for some time over the first face they had ever seen – gone – gone – the great system within that once living entity called Mai'O'Mai would never be again.

AO: This is terrible. What are the Po'Pitians supposed to do now?

ODOM: They are supposed to heed Mai'O'Mai's warning. They are supposed to learn as a people.

AO: Do they?

CHAPTER 4 - LASTING WORDS

One night, a few years later, from out of a fit-filled slumber, Blu'Bla shot awake. They had the answer. They had to tell the others – everyone had to know. Quickly they rolled out of their chamber and into the halls. They rolled to the Mapping Den where Trudge and several youths were posted in their absence. And they said, "The asteroids!"

Trudge and the youths stood there scratching their heads. "The asteroids?" Asked the Hull Monitor.

"Yes!" Shouted Blu'Bla, "Bigger things! Mai'O'Mai's final words held our answer. They have saved us again!"

Blu'Bla was so excited, but the others still didn't understand.

One of the youths even said, "What are you talking about, elder?"

So Blu'Bla pulled up the folded projection of the star map and the path of trash. Ark ship Po'Pito was represented there as well as a host of additional celestial bodies. "The ship needs to ingest 'Bigger Things' – the asteroid belt." They pointed at the large space rocks not too far from the course the path of trash led them along. "We can create a sturdier hull by allowing the ship to eat more! Then we can awaken as many limbs as we need to without running out of food! Heck, even the ship might indigest faster…"

The den was silent as everyone contemplated Blu'Bla's words. Eventually, Trudge asked, "Is this thing possible?"

"Sure," replied the maven. "We just change course a few degrees every so often… steer into the asteroids and then back onto the path… No harm done."

"Steer?" Asked Trudge again.

"Blu'Bla's right," said young Syk'Ry who had already gained quite the reputation in his first few years of living. "We can recalibrate the tufts of propulsion by folding the exhaust components from inside the ship. With just the right wrinkle in exactly the right spot, we could change direction more consistently without the fear of losing our course." Syk'Ry drew their plan out so the group could see.

And Blu'Bla chuckled and said, "Smart kid."

"We should get on this right away," added Trudge. And the whole crew got to work – Blu'Bla informing the rest of the ship about the plan – creating a sense of relief for a people on edge since the passing of their most beloved savior – finally someone had figured this thing out – Mai'O'Mai's great conundrum solved – and they all could go on living in this, actually rather comfortable, ark ship for as long as the journey required. Well, for almost that long.

AO: Wait, could they not steer before?

ODOM: *It's complicated, but essentially, before Blu'Bla's and Syk'Ry's suggestions, no one had actually needed to. The path of trash was a long, straight line. Only when the ship would veer slightly, would some recalibrating be required, but the wrinkling process Syk'Ry devised was their first great contribution to the Po'Pitian story. So I've made sure to include it here alongside Blu'Bla's own discovery, as it should be.*

AO: *I'm glad we're getting to see Syk'Ry.*

ODOM: *I know, Ao.*

CHAPTER 5 - A NEW WRINKLE

With the exhaust thruster manipulating by a series of preassigned wrinkles, the ark ship Po'Pito had become a fine-tuned, high-functioning, steering machine. Indeed, the Po'Pitians could maneuver their vessel in any direction they liked, and while they remained partial to sticking nearby the trail of garbage as insisted upon by the late Mai'O'Mai, it became a new sort of game for the youths to devise the best route off of and back onto that long, seemingly never ending line. Syk'Ry and their best buddies, Lou'Gi and Gum'Gum, would choose the objects worth changing course for, map out the new trajectory, show their plan to the old brain trust, and once approval was granted, they would steer the ark ship onto a direct collision course with that celestial body. Whenever possible, Blu'Bla would come down to the Mapping Den to lay witness to the amazing event with the youths. One moment the projection of stars would show a massive asteroid beside the ark ship, the next, it would be gone. This would always bring a tear to the maven's eye – the consumption stage. After, Trudge would draw core samples from the inner walls as they always had proving that the hull was strong as ever, and for nearly three hundred years, life carried on in this way – the youthful limbs growing into full maturity, the brain trust becoming genuine elders.

AO: They were in the ark ship for so long, Odom.

ODOM: This is a fair assessment of the situation. Yes, in human terms, the Po'Pitians lived on their ark ship for several lifetimes. But, in Po'Pitian terms, it would have been less than one.

There came a day, about three hundred and thirty-seven years into the voyage, when the map showed signs of a new, strangely shaped heap of space debris a little farther off the beaten path than the refugee ship would usually travel. When Syk'Ry caught a glimpse of this new, strange and variable collection of shapes, they insisted it would be worth passing through that way. Over a few short days they corroborated their plan with Lou'Gi and Gum'Gum. Once all had been diametrically mapped for tangent and return to the line of the ship, Syk'Ry approached Blu'Bla and Bir'Do at the Garden in earnest. "I'd like to venture out in the direction of this cluster of celestial bodies," they said. "But I don't think we should allow the ship to eat whatever they are until we get a better look at them."

"A wise plan, Syk'Ry," said Blu'Bla, hoping to give full acceptance to the plan right then and there, "You really are your parent's limb – from the same stalk as Fa'Mica."

But Bir'Do had become religiously devoted to the cause of expansion. In their old age they had become as immovable as a mountain range. "I do not see the merit in this, young Syk'Ry. What would be the point of not allowing the ship to feed on these new materials?"

"Discovery," argued Syk'Ry, "Exploration."

"Push posh," answered the Keeper of the Garden. "I would not vote for such an endeavor. The ship needs to eat. Such a wide berth away from the trail would set us back many days. I will not be made responsible should this force us to put a pause on the upcoming awakenings."

"But—" said Syk'Ry.

"But," answered Blu'Bla, "we will call upon Trudge then. They shall be the final vote as is custom."

So Trudge was called into the Garden. They were informed of the arguments but not told in which direction each of the others had voted. And in the end, they chose the side of ingesting the new materials, for they too had grown fearful of Mai'O'Mai's predictions; set in their ways.

AO: They voted to eat the new objects without investigating? I don't get it.

ODOM; Often times, elders can lose sight of the possibilities of new discovery. Habit and an echo chamber of rhetoric and fear can leave them with no clear thoughts of their own. And if such individuals are allowed to remain in leadership positions, they can stall societal progress as we are witnessing here.

AO: But that's still two votes to two. They should obviously investigate.

ODOM: Ah, but that is where you are wrong, Ao. You miscount. Syk'Ry did not yet hold a vote with the brain trust.

AO: Why not?

ODOM: Because, old ways die hard.

AO: That's dumb.

ODOM: Yes, we are in agreement on that.

Regardless, the plan of ingesting the new cluster of celestial bodies moved forward. And, at first, Bir'Do and Trudge seemed to be proven correct in their assertions to feed. The younger crew still had an opportunity to briefly study the strange new formations and the ship wasted no time in ingesting the shapes and moving back to the long trail of garbage. Trudge's core samples were impeccable and no awakenings would have to be postponed or cancelled.

But then, several days later, something unfathomable happened. The trail of garbage ended suddenly. The ark ship Po'Pito was rudderless, floating loosely in space without direction. Panic set in and the brain trust and the young crew met again in the Mapping Den one more time to argue.

"There is a great object nearby," said Syk'Ry. "Bigger even than our ship. We should try to explore it."

"We should try to eat it," said Bir'Do.

"We would not be able to fit something so massive into the mouth of the ship," Blu'Bla insisted. "Perhaps it is time we attempt to come to ground."

"Sheer nonsense," argued Bir'Do. "Why should we ever leave this ship? It's so cozy in here."

"Because," answered Blu'Bla, "we will run out of food in short order as Mai'O'Mai once predicted."

"Bla bla bla, Blu'Bla," quipped the Keeper of the Garden.

And Trudge said, "There is another small object. We could eat that couldn't we?"

Syk'Ry looked up at the projection to see what Trudge was talking about. Where a moment ago there had only been one large object floating there before them, now there was in fact a tiny blip as well. And, oddly enough, it seemed to move in their direction intentionally. They need not even adjust the thruster wrinkles to steer toward it.

"Yes," replied Bir'Do. "This is a fine idea. Let's eat it."

But then the small blip split into ten small blips and, all at once, the blips collided with the hull of the ark ship Po'Pito.

AO: What?!

A large rupture formed in one of the halls just outside the Mapping Den and the expanse of space reflected against the naked eyes of the six Po'Pitians there. Bir'Do and Trudge were the first to be sucked out into the cold – approximately negative two hundred seventy point five five six degrees celsius – colder than a silicone based rock person can survive.

AO: They died too?!

Blu'Bla grasped against a cleave in the slate of the Mapping Den with one arm and caught Syk'Ry with the other. Syk'Ry caught Lou'Gi and Lou'Gi caught Gum'Gum. And, as a team, the four of them struggled to push against the door to the next hall over and worked their way inside the sealable corridor. How many had been lost alongside Bir'Do and Trudge? Only time would tell.

AO: I don't understand. What just happened? What hit them?

SEVENTH INTERLUDE

THE BROKEN ARROWS OF TIME

Earth - Better Days

The projection ceased. Ao was alone in the library fumbling her body in her seat out of extreme discomfort. Odom had been gone for longer than usual between lessons. His light was not even present in that strange drippy thing up top from what Ao could tell as she craned her neck to try and see. "Odom?" Asked the girl after the short hiatus had become too much for her. "Odom, I don't understand. What's going on right now?"

Odom's orb whipped around the corner then. He seemed… impossibly… out of breath. "My apologies, Ao," he said.

Behind the orb, a rack of additional records rolled into the room – the cartridges of data and stored memory rattling as they approached.

"Where did you go just now, Odom?" Ao was noticeably flustered by the proceedings. Something cruel and unexpected had just happened in Blu'Bla's story and she couldn't seem to find a good place to put her attention.

Slowly, the hard drives rose up from the rack and cubbied themselves within one of the library's receptor points. "I had to retrieve the next lesson. It is no longer a piece of cumulative memory from the Po'Pitian species, and while my own perspective might have given a decent account of the comings and goings of Adonis, I feared that without a bit more datum to correlate with, my own sense of time as it hinges in your universe might have seemed… distracted."

"Adonis?" Ao asked with confusion, "Odom, what are you talking about? Why would your sense of time be a problem?"

Odom's orb stopped shuffling and all of the technology from the rolling rack sat still in place at last. "We will come to a deeper explanation in short order," said the computer, "but for now, let it suffice to be said that many things happened between the time of the Save Our Space initiative on Adonis and the ark ship Po'Pito's arrival within that region of space."

"So that bigger object the Po'Pitians had seen before the explosion… that was Adonis?" Ao looked completely gobsmacked as she said this.

"That is correct," reflected the computer.

"But," Ao lingered on the thought, "It didn't look anything like Adonis from the Mapping Den."

"That is precisely the reason I had to collect additional materials, Ao," said Odom. "I wish to give you a more full accounting of the events on the planet Adonis in the time before the Po'Pitian hull was breeched."

Ao shook her head. "What were all those blips on the map, Odom?"

"I shall show you in the following lesson," Odom replied. "We can begin right away. That is, if you are not too tired, Ao? I know it has been a long and eventful day for you."

"I mean, yeah," answered the girl, "I'm tired, but I don't wanna have nightmares again, Odom. That explosion was terrible. I didn't wanna see Trudge and Bir'Do get sucked out into space like that… no matter how much they were acting like a couple of buttheads by the end."

"If it helps you to make a decision," considered Odom, "we will review that explosion in the midst of the coming lesson. But it will not be the stopping point. I have reason to believe the thoughts we will conclude upon tonight will not give course to any more bad dreams should you choose to continue. Though I am not a human and, at times, my understanding of such things can be flawed." Odom watched Ao whose discomfort was obviously growing in that moment. "I shall leave the decision in your hands, Ao. Carry on for one more lesson, or slumber."

Ao weighed her options. "If I sleep now, I know I'm gonna have another bad dream. If I don't and the Adonis lesson is terrible… well, I don't think my mind would be in a worse state than it already is at the moment."

"Such is the conundrum of choice," Odom hummed, "time's broken arrows branching off in so very many directions – none of these can ever be predicted in full no matter the evidence we have at hand."

"You're a lot like Pauline, you know that, Odom?" The girl told him.

"Whatever do you mean, Ao?" Asked the computer.

"You're like a poet sometimes," said the girl. "That last thing you said was really pretty."

"It was?" Asked the computer – a little embarrassed.

"It was," said Ao. "Okay, I feel better about the idea of trusting your judgement. If you say it's gonna end better with this lesson," she yawned briefly, "I wanna hear it tonight. If you turn out to be wrong, I was gonna sleep bad after that explosion anyway."

"Very well," said Odom. "Let's begin right away then, shall we?"

BOOK VIII

WISCONSIN NULL AND CHERRY BLOSSOM

Adonis - The Number Affair and the thousandth year after

CHAPTER 1 - THE W ENCYCLOPEDIA

It had not been long since Ariko Sevenson had taken her team into space to clear away the nearby garbage trailing off of Papillon IV. Only about one hundred years…

AO: Odom, a hundred years is a long time.
ODOM: For an individual human, certainly.

…and the world of Adonis had plodded along on its course toward complete independence from all of the other humans around the galaxy. The Numbers kept a strict record of the planet's cleaning processes among their other documents and ensured that a subclass of the population whose ancestors had ranked in the upper teens aboard Papillon I would always be available in the event of a spill or a broken piece of pavement or the like. Where these Teens' progenitors had taken the ark ship and travelled to Adonis seeking out a better life, those born on the planet had essentially been forced into indentured servitude by the single digit Numbers of the world.

AO: What's indentured servitude mean, Odom?
ODOM: Slavery… When one's life is not their own.

Wiskay Teenine was one such individual living in that state of lower class slavery on the world of Adonis a hundred years after Save Our Space. Wiskay Teenine was a strong man with callused hands and a sore lower body as he had to squat most days to wipe away whatever scum the neighboring Eighters left in their tracks as they walked from laboratory to laboratory. Wiskay had often dreamed of being involved in the important experiments of the day, but the closest he had ever come to the Eighters' compelling work was on cleanup duty. Every single day of the lower ranked man's life, he had to squat and clean and watch as those Eighters found genuine meaning in their work. Oh, it wasn't that the cleaning didn't have merit, but Wiskay wanted more than the planet seemed willing to offer him. And the other Numbers never much cared what mess they were making, so Wiskay never really could find the time he so desperately wanted to simply sit back and contemplate his circumstances.

That is, until the centennial anniversary of Cleanup Day – Ariko the 115th on the Adonian calendar. Usually on Cleanup Day, it had become custom for all of the Numbers regardless of rank to do a little bit more… essentially the Single Digits would take part in cleanup duties and the Teens would be granted an easier go of things. In fact, usually on this day, people would actually think about what mess they were making since they knew they would have to help the Teens, so they simply wouldn't leave rubbish lying around in the same way they usually had.

But this centennial anniversary was different. The Single Digits had planned a huge celebration event... it was an important day in their history after all... the day Adonis had taken a stand and removed the last dregs of their former Earth history from the records alongside all of that trash in space.

> *AO: Are you saying the Adonians had erased their records of Earth altogether when Ariko flew around in space near Papillon IV?*
>
> *ODOM: Yes. That is part of what makes this lesson so cumbersome. We must piece together the broken records of Adonis with visual elements that I can only partly see from witnessed Nexus accounts.*
>
> *AO: O...kay... so what happened next?*

Instead of his usual breather of a day, on the centennial of Ariko, Wiskay was forced to work extra. The celebration plans had grown so overwhelmingly decadent that the Single Digits actually left an even greater mess than on a normal day. And, unfortunately, as Wiskay Teenine scrubbed and scrubbed and removed the overabundance of waste, he slipped and fell off of a celebration platform and broke his back.

> *AO: Oh no! Odom, how is this supposed to be better? The Adonians sound just as terrible as the ones on Earth that they were trying to get away from.*

The humans of Adonis did have the necessary technology and medical knowhow to repair Whiskey's broken back. But as he was a subservient, not all steps were taken in the same fashion as if he were, say, an Eighter. So Wiskay's days transformed from long, strenuous, literally backbreaking work into agonizing, bedridden discomfort and, when not heavily drugged, extreme boredom. He did not have many visitors during this time as most of his friends were stuck out and about performing their regular, meticulous cleaning duties.

However, as these awkward days of inactivity progressed, Wiskay's mind was finally allowed to wander since he had little else to occupy himself away from his thoughts. It was either that or watch mind numbing soap operas about petty Single Digits or other terrible daytime television. Wiskay opted for his thoughts over either. When the pain was not too great, he would contemplate the nature of his life on Adonis… how unfair it was that some should be born to serve while others were allowed to lead and grow their minds. He often found himself wondering why his birth number should have been a factor at all. He could be a critical thinker, he decided, better than those who were currently in charge.

One day, Wiskay Teenine's nurse came in during an hour when the man was still awake… It was a rather uncommon practice for one so far down the list to actually receive face time with a medical professional.

> *AO: They wouldn't even see him when he was awake?*
> *ODOM: He was not deemed important enough for*
> *genuine nurse communication, no.*
> *AO: I really don't like this planet.*
> *ODOM: This is an understandable assessment.*

The nurse, a man named Robby Elevenen, did not flee when he realized his mistake of walking in on a lower ranked person who was currently awake. To his credit, Robby said, "Hello." And he asked, "How is your day going…" he checked his medical chart and read out the name, "…Mr. Teenine?"

"Back still hurts," grumbled the patient.

"I am sorry to hear that. Would you like some more numbing agent?"

"No," pled Wiskay. "No. Please, no. I'd like to feel… I am bored though."

"Television?" Robby asked delicately. The nurse's bedside manner when he actually could be gotten in the room was not unkind. "There's a great new series on the intricacies of the production of aquavit on the optionals–"

"No no," Wiskay responded again. "I've heard enough about aquavit to last a hundred lifetimes."

"Is that so?" Asked the nurse rhetorically. "How about a documentary on electrical engineering?"

"I think…" Wiskay plodded through the thought, his mind terribly fuzzy at the moment. "Might there be anything to read…?"

It was an odd request to be sure. Books had long ago been discarded as a medium in favor of digitized content… which someone in Wiskay's rank could not afford. Regardless, Robby Elevenen did take the man's request to heart. He stepped out into the hallway and opened a closet that he had known still contained some of those old paper and ink items. Grabbing at one of the volumes, Robby returned to Wiskay's room and presented the man with the W Encyclopedia. "W," he said, "for Wiskay." Robby Elevenen smiled and left the room.

What the nurse hadn't understood about that encyclopedia was its otherworldly origin. You see, though the Numbers had erased any memory of Earth from their digital platforms, they had not thought it necessary to seek out physical books. Who would care to read them? Besides, most of those books had become too worn out across the voyage of time as to have still been considered legible… and that was more than a hundred years before this particular moment. That W Encyclopedia was actually one of the most impressively conserved volumes on all of Adonis. And Wiskay Teenine became obsessed with its contents over the next several months.

CHAPTER 2 - WORDS TO WALK AWAY WITH

Rummaging delicately through the ancient encyclopedia, Wiskay came across an entry on the old state of Wisconsin. Something in that name grew on the man. He had never truly connected with his own namesake very greatly as he was not a particularly consistent drinker. And, for what it was worth, he no longer wished to go by his slave moniker of Teenine either. So he decided to reinvent himself in one fell swoop. And, though the public records would not recognize the new name for another three hundred years, a fully grown, adult man named Wisconsin Null was born in that hospital bed, molded out of the pain that Wiskay Teenine had suffered.

Wisconsin Null learned about ancient Earth history, about World Wars and West Nile virus, about the people of Wales and West Virginia, about men named Wilhelm and Washington. He became obsessed with these seemingly fictitious facts. And he remade his world view around the strange lessons they had to teach him.

One day, the new man named Wisconsin Null stood up on his own two feet and walked right out of that hospital, his back fully healed and his mind filled with anti-Adonian ideals.

The Eighters put Wisconsin Null up in a government dormitory. He could stay there under the condition that he would rejoin the work force when his body had healed more fully. Wisconsin Null made certain that such a thing never would come to pass.

> *AO: He wouldn't go back to work?*
> *ODOM: Would you if you felt, as he did, that you were being oppressed?*
> *AO: I dunno. What's oppressed mean?*
> *ODOM: Oppression is when an individual or group is deemed lesser than by another individual or faction. Usually the term applies to those who are not granted the same rights as others or are unjustly imprisoned or mistreated.*
> *AO: Oh. I guess probably not.*

He wouldn't go back to work, but Wisconsin Null would seek out other Teenines and Teeneights so that he might share his discoveries with them. And, slowly but surely, a new, secret order began to follow this man. They called themselves the Defiant Teens.

CHAPTER 3 - THE DEFIANT TEENS

In their sole year together, Wisconsin and the Defiant Teens mounted a rather intense series of subterfuges against the Numbers. Walkouts (another lesson from the encyclopedia) became a prominent form of protest within their ranks and often the Single Digits would come back from a lunch or an aquavit session to find their work spaces in utter disarray... What the Single Digits always failed to recognize during all of this was that such messes had already been there before they left... of their own making. Instead, the Eighters and their like assumed someone was deliberately messing up their work stations while they were away... an assertion that any video records remaining from that age have long since proven false.

But a ruling class often invents excuses or attempts to change the narrative. The Numbers tried to vilify Wisconsin and his companions, painting them as terrorists intent on destroying the Adonian way of life. In truth, Wisconsin was simply mounting a totally legal strike... but such an event had not been anticipated by the Adonians who had so meticulously planned for every other eventuality. The very idea that a citizen of Adonis would even desire a different political order in their life seemed – to the lawmakers – utterly inconceivable.

AO: But Odom, isn't that exactly how Adonis was founded in the first place?

ODOM: Explain your assertion please, Ao.

AO: Well, if the people who populated Adonis originally left Earth because they didn't like the way things were going there… didn't that essentially mean they were also 'walking out'… also on strike?

ODOM: Very good, Ao. Yes, this is an excellent comparison.

AO: So how come they didn't think about someone else doing it to them when they, as a people, had already shown themselves to be capable of something like that?

ODOM: A very good question. Unfortunately, my best answer is most humans have a genetically ingrained survival mechanism within their DNA that specifically makes them forget traumatic events so they may continue on with their lives without forcing greater mental stress upon themselves. In this way, many humans are surprisingly prone to missing the most basic of facts. Sometimes those facts sit physically right in front of their eyes and are subconsciously avoided. Often this is why solutions to some of life's biggest mysteries seem to allude the human species for far longer than they should. This is why it is so important that your species continue to reach out for help… whether it be other biological species that harbor the answers they seek… or entities such as myself that exist beyond the boundaries of previously known space. Anyway…

One day, Wisconsin Null was arrested alongside a band of his closest Defiants. He was brought to trial for his terrorist crimes. It was during these proceedings – televised for all the population of the planet Adonis to see – that Wisconsin was allowed to present his own video evidence of the state of the Eighters' labs to the world. He was allowed to tell the people why he had mounted resistance to the state of his rank and station. And then, he was promptly executed for his crimes against humanity.

AO: They executed him?!

ODOM: They did, Ao.

AO: But he didn't do anything!

ODOM: Precisely. Wisconsin Null did nothing. And according to Adonian politics at that time, 'Nothing' was considered a pock on society. To do 'Nothing' was treated as the greatest of all possible crimes. The penalty for Wisconsin Null was death. But he became a symbol to many others who came after. And over the next thousand years, the people of Adonis learned from his peaceful example.

CHAPTER 4 - THE CLASSROOM, THE SATELLITE, THE SKY

A thousand years later, a girl named Cherry Blossom sat in a classroom learning about the Defiant Teens of all those years ago – how, with their sacrifice, they brought to light the injustices of the time and ultimately led the planet Adonis toward a new age of 'Human Equality.' However, that last statement is still somewhat debatable to this day. But, for what it was worth, many more voices were allowed to be heard in public forums across that world without the fear of repercussions to an individual's social wellbeing.

Cherry Blossom was a kind, eight-year-old and – though she did not know it yet – she was a descendent of Ariko Sevenson. As she sat in her classroom of about twenty-five students, she watched the presented video of Wisconsin Null's final argument. What the man had said a thousand years prior was this: "It is not I who causes you such turmoil. It is yourselves. Should you look hard in the mirror and see a person who is without guilt for standing on the throats of an underclass, I can only commend your ugliness. For there is none in this world who is without guilt. There is none who has not run away from the blight of their own ancestors. And there is none who has genuinely allowed fairness and equality into their hearts. While in my hospital bed recovering from an injury provoked upon me only by the laziness of the Single Digits, I learned of the place from which our ancestors so nonchalantly sought to escape. I learned that we are headed down the same terrible road as that other planet and those other but same people. Can we not take the evidence this time and learn from those mistakes? If we cannot, our roads and our crops will become equally littered. Our own descendants will blame us in kind for the same blight. This is a cycle that should not and cannot continue."

To Cherry Blossom and the millions of students who had watched this video over the past thousand years, Wisconsin's words became a terrible prophecy fulfilled. You see, Adonis had changed after the actions of the Defiant Teens. But, perhaps, not in the way anyone should have hoped. A light had been shined upon the underbelly of society. And, once the Single Digits were made to understand the social injustices they had committed, their own take on leadership changed. Gone were the days of extra planning and forced conservation. All were deemed allowed to follow whatever path they sought. And for many, that path was to follow in Wisconsin's footsteps and do 'nothing.' Population became a problem – litter, a constant thing to step around on those once pristine streets – and for Cherry Blossom and her generation, already the thing their great great great great (etc) grand parents had hoped to protect them from had slipped away almost entirely.

AO: *Is that why there were so many kids in her classroom, Odom?*

ODOM: *Would you say there were?*

AO: *I mean, twenty-five's a lot of kids.*

ODOM: *True. Though there were closer to forty children in Pauline Delgado's classroom if you'll recall.*

AO: *Yeah, but wasn't that an example of a planet that had already passed its available population limits?*

ODOM: *Yes. Forty students were certainly too many. Similarly, you are correct in assuming that twenty-five children in one classroom would be too many to accomplish the necessary task of education in a just and genuine fashion as well. I'm very proud of you, Ao.*

AO: *Why?*

ODOM: *Because you are drawing meaningful conclusions from the evidence presented in these lessons. Even, sometimes, lessons that I did not intend to expose you to yet have already become apparent facts that you have managed to puzzle out of the minutia.*

AO: *Minutia?*

ODOM: *Small, trivially unimportant details...*

Cherry Blossom sat there among her class of twenty-five listening to Wisconsin Null's words and knowing in her eight-year-old heart that the worst of them had already come to pass. She struggled to sit still for the rest of the period, fidgeting in her seat all the while as her teacher tried to work out additional aspects of the history lesson that were quickly lost on the girl.

When class ended, Cherry Blossom did not stay to chat with her friend group as she usually was apt to do. Instead, she jumped into the first sun bus available and took the vehicle home where maybe she could find some peace of mind. Cherry Blossom's home was in the reconstructed quarter of her town. At one time, these homes were seen as symbols of the greatness and generosity of the Single Digits, built solely from materials that had been scrapped off of Papillon I. But that too was well over a thousand years ago. And the houses had since gone through many phases of scrap and repair until far more of them resembled metaphorical camels built with bored and mined Adonian materials rather than the metaphorical horses they were meant to be.

AO: Camels? Horses?
ODOM: This is a camel and this is a horse.
AO: That's funny. They look so different but…
ODOM: Precisely.

The eight-year-old girl arrived in her messy, makeshift home to find her father asleep in a chair with the television on. The man had not been able to find a decent line of work for quite some time and it was not abnormal for him to be found taking long naps rather than, say, cleaning up the house, or preparing the family meal. He had clearly taken Wisconsin's doctrine as a fair excuse not to be a productive or helpful member of society. And, knowing this, it is rather impressive to find that Cherry Blossom was such an optimist most of the time. But, of course, on this day she was upset. She came inside and sat down beside her snoring father and hoped to let the television drain away this new feeling of sorrow that had overtaken her during the Wisconsin Null lesson.

Fortunately, however, she did not fall asleep or zone out too drastically during the next hour because, on that Adonian television, a Special Emergency Report took over on all the major broadcasters. The words "Massive Unidentified Object Destroys Government Satellite" were displayed along the top of the screen.

"Da," Cherry Blossom said as she tried to nudge her father awake.

He said, "Peace and love, Cherry Blossom. I'm only sleeping a little while."

"No Da," insisted the girl, "look at the feed."

Her father opened his eyes groggily and caught a glimpse of the insane report. "What's that supposed to mean, baby girl?"

"I dunno, Da," Cherry Blossom replied.

Together, they and millions of Adonians watched the slow burn of that news cycle. Whatever the object was up there, it was massive and powerful... and it certainly did not seem friendly. After all, it had just destroyed a government probe satellite. Only something with malicious intent would do something like that... or at least that's how the reports ran —

the entire planet of Adonis already an echo chamber of xenophobia.

> *AO: What's xenophobia, Odom?*
> *ODOM: Dislike or fear of another race or species,*
>   *usually based on ignorant or unfoundable biases.*
> *AO: Oh okay. That makes sense. Hey, Odom?*
> *ODOM: Yes, Ao?*
> *AO: Is that Po'Pito up there that just destroyed that*
>   *satellite?*
> *ODOM: Yes, Ao. How very astute of you.*

"Da, do you think they're gonna…" Cherry Blossom wavered as she asked, "are we gonna try to communicate with that thing?"

"I dunno, baby girl," answered the father. "I'm sure somebody's got a contingency plan for stuff like this. The Numbers used to have a plan for everything."

"But Da, that was a long time ago," rebutted the girl.

"Sure," contemplated the father, "but it's not like those plans got up and walked away or something. Honestly, you can probably find them in the Public Archive."

Cherry Blossom didn't sleep well that night. On more than one occasion, she had to get out of bed to stretch her legs. Each time, she used this as a subconscious excuse to step out onto their worn out, old patio to glance up at the night's sky. As she stood there in the cool, dry air of the moonless dusk, she imagined she could see the shadow of that mysterious craft lingering over her. She wondered, eyes to the unobstructed stars, what such a massive space ship might actually want out of her world. Were they enemy or friend? Perhaps, even they did not know.

> AO: They didn't know, Odom. The Po'Pitians didn't even understand what they were looking at when they ate that satellite.
>
> ODOM: Correct. Still, it is always a good practice for us to attempt to see both perspectives in a conflict.
>
> AO: Why?
>
> ODOM: Because, Ao, often that is how we can discover a solution.

CHAPTER 5 - CONTINGENCY AND THE PUBLIC ARCHIVE

Cherry Blossom sat at her desk in class the next day wondering dreamily about the events of the night before. So was every other child in the school to be honest. All of the teachers had come to the firm conclusion that the incident of the massive object destroying the government satellite should be considered 'history in the making.' And, as such, every classroom allowed the daily news cycle to stream on their projectors and televisions rather than teaching their potentially outdated curriculums. In fact, hardly any work at all was getting done planet wide. The only people really putting in any work on that day were those in the various space-related agencies of government and the broadcasters following them through their morbid debates. The primary arguments made during the news cycle were based around how best to defend the planet from these potential invaders – how to strike back. And

Cherry Blossom was acutely aware that not a one of the politicians on hand had argued the case of attempting to make contact with the aliens before other actions might be taken.

She raised her hand and asked, "Mr. Diode, may I be excused early today?"

Mr. Diode, her teacher, had been just as enthralled with the reports on the television as everyone else. He didn't even turn his head to see who had been speaking as he waved her off and said, "Sure sure," between a set of heavy, anxious breaths.

Getting up from her seat, Cherry Blossom eyed her friend Tom Tom and the young boy rose from his seat asking, "Can I go too, Mr. Diode?"

Again, the breathy, dispossessed, "Sure sure," echoed hollowly from the front of the room.

So the two children exited the classroom and walked quietly through the hallways until they passed through the front doors of the school. Only once they were outside did Tom Tom think to ask, "What is it, Cherry Blossom? It's not like we were being forced to learn statistics or something today."

"No, it's not that, Tom Tom," answered Cherry Blossom in contemplation. "It's just, I think something bad's about to happen."

"Duh," said the boy. "A giant alien ship's coming to blow us all up... or enslave us... or eat us or something. You ever hear about that book from the W Encyclopedia that Wisconsin used to pull his info from... *War of the Worlds*? Wasn't that about aliens harvesting people like crops or something?"

Cherry Blossom was annoyed. "I don't know about all that, Tom Tom. But how are we supposed to find out what the aliens want if no one's even a little bit willing to try and talk to them in the first place?"

Tom Tom didn't have an answer to that question. Instead, he huffed and shrugged his shoulders on repeat for a full minute.

"Can we just go do what I was trying to do in the first place?" Cherry Blossom put her hand on Tom Tom's arm. "I promise it's not gonna be scary or anything."

The boy blushed. "Okay. What's the plan, Cherry?"

"I wanna go to the Public Archive," said the girl.

"You wanna skip school to go do a boring school field trip?"

"No, stupid boy," Cherry Blossom shook her head. "I want to find out what the Numbers would have done in this instance. None of the talking heads have even mentioned the old contingency records even once in all of this."

"That's cause the Numbers were a bunch of ruthless oligarchs," rebutted Tom Tom. "Why should anybody care what they would've had to say about it?"

"Because… what if attacking the aliens only makes things worse?" Asked Cherry Blossom crudely. "Wouldn't it be better if we tried peace before violence?"

"Peace before violence," repeated Tom Tom slowly. "They already destroyed that satellite, didn't they?"

"Was anyone hurt?"

Silence from the boy who knew he was wrong.

"Tom Tom," Cherry Blossom repeated, "was anybody hurt? Have the aliens shown any other actual signs of hostility?"

"I'm talking to a crazy person," Tom Tom said to himself. "Okay, sure, let's go look into it."

"Thanks," Cherry Blossom hugged Tom Tom and the boy's cheeks went full red.

Together, the two eight-year-olds rode the next sun bus to the Public Archives. Everyone traveling that day was glued to their personal devices watching the same news cycle as the pundits talked themselves into greater and worse ways of striking back against the alien aggressors. And, unfortunately, the politicians seemed to agree. Something bad was going to happen. But that didn't stop Cherry Blossom from her mission. Her father always said, "Peace and Love." That's the person she wanted to be even if she had to do it in her own way.

The doors to the sun bus opened and the kids got off at the hodgepodge Public Archives building. It was old and musty with bad patch jobs and expansions in awkward places... a lot like the houses on Cherry Blossom's block but with the failed intention of being somewhat grander in scale and more accommodating.

As Cherry Blossom and Tom Tom entered the old museum of records it was eerily clear that no one meant to be working was at their post. Apparently, even these resource gatekeepers felt the broadcasts were more important on this particular day. So the children began wandering through the many narrow halls.

"How are we supposed to know where to look?" Tom Tom asked in a whisper.

Cherry Blossom pointed up to the extremely legible sign that said 'Numbers Wing' with a clear arrow pointing down the next hallway. "The signs," she replied dryly.

"Oh," said Tom Tom, "that's pretty convenient actually."

"Right?" Said Cherry Blossom. "It is supposed to be a resource for learning after all. Things are supposed to be easy to find."

"That's fair, I guess," said Tom Tom.

They turned down the marked hallway into the Numbers Wing. Within, there was a display of an odd, human-sized orb that looked like it had fallen into an active volcano. Beyond that were a bunch of projector screens repetitively showing off footage of the Papillon I landing and the founding days of Adonis. Old political figures speaking on mute with subtitles so others wouldn't be disturbed by the speeches.

Cherry Blossom turned another corner and finally saw what she came for… The section for opened letters and computer diagrams labelled 'Contingency.' It was a lot to take in all at once with some letters plastered all the way up onto the ceiling and others lacquered into the floor. Tom Tom joined her saying, "What the…?"

"It's a mess," Cherry Blossom said in awe and confusion.

"How are we supposed to find anything in all this jumble?" Tom Tom asked.

"I don't know." Cherry Blossom looked over to the first eye level spread of articles on her left. "I'll start over here… you look on that side." She pointed at the other wall.

"But…" Tom Tom shook his head but did as Cherry Blossom asked anyway.

AO: Why did the Adonians display the letters like that, Odom?

ODOM: Consider, Ao, that the people of that world looked on the Numbers as people of Earth may look on the Romans of old. Their doctrine was considered cruel and antiquated. So these articles of contingency were thought merely relics of another age. Just something to display for school students to look at during their field trips. Somewhere along the line, someone had thought it would look impressive if presented in papier-mâché. They had long ago stopped considering that anyone might actually want to read those words.

AO: Ugh, people are so dumb sometimes.

Cherry Blossom read page after page all the way down the hall — things like 'Should an active fault line become evident near an encampment, first test the size of the fissure with a good meter stick…' or 'When blight comes for the caraway crop, quarantine the area in question so the illness does not spread, then expunge the sickly plants with fire and apply anti-fungals to the soil there.' All very interesting sentiments, to be sure, but none of the eye-level articles held an answer to the girl's current question. And Tom Tom's side was seemingly taking twice as long. He had stopped halfway down the hall and lingered there in the middle.

"Hey, Tom Tom," said Cherry Blossom from the far side of the room, "you find anything yet?" She approached the boy adding, "My first round didn't have anything about space ships or..." She stopped speaking. As she had come closer to her friend, she realized that he wasn't even trying to read the articles on the walls any longer. He held a streaming device in his far hand keeping his back intentionally to the girl. And he had headphones in. Tom Tom was watching the news just like everyone else. "Tom Tom..." Cherry Blossom tapped his shoulder and the boy jumped knowing he had been caught.

"Sorry, Cherry," he pled. "This place is just so boring."

"No it's not," Cherry Blossom replied. "You just don't get it."

Tom Tom shuffled around awkwardly. He really hadn't expected his friend to catch him splitting his attention.

AO: Tom Tom's a jerk.
ODOM: Well...

As Tom Tom shuffled his feet around he noticed the word 'Extraterrestrial" in one of the articles lacquered to the floor just beneath him. "Did you see this, Cherry?" He asked kneeling down to get a better look.

Cherry Blossom joined him on hands and knees. "That's... this is it."

The article began 'If Extraterrestrials should enter into Adonian space without prior communication, first..." but the next series of words were buried beneath another batch of letters.

"What's it say?" Tom Tom asked.

"I don't know. It's blocked," Cherry Blossom responded. Thinking quickly, she added, "We've gotta get it out of the floor."

"We've gotta... What?" Tom Tom was not particularly rebellious and it showed.

"Come on," the girl started clawing at the clear material holding the articles in place, but the lacquer wouldn't budge against her fingernails. "We need, like, a knife or something."

"Are you serious?" Asked the boy.

"Yeah," said Cherry Blossom, "do you have anything in your bag we could use, Tom Tom?"

"We just came from school, Cherry," answered Tom Tom. "I'm not in the habit of illegally sneaking knives into classrooms."

"Okay okay, I get the point," Cherry Blossom rolled her eyes. "What else can we use?" She got up and looked around. Back over by the projectors, someone had installed an old meter stick into a display. "Stay there so we don't lose the spot, okay?"

Tom Tom nodded and Cherry Blossom walked over to grasp the thin old tool. Glancing up at the moving images in that room, she saw a woman getting into a spherical pod and flying up into space.

AO: That was Ariko!
ODOM: Indeed it was, Ao.

Cherry Blossom watched as Ariko Sevenson performed her space walk around Papillon IV. She glanced over at the old, scorched orb at the front of the Numbers wing and then back at the image of the pod on the screen. They were the same.

"Cherry!" Tom Tom was calling for her from the other hallway.

She turned her attention back to her friend. Plucking the meter stick from the wall, she rejoined him noticing that he was fully invested in his own streaming device again. "What is it, Tom Tom?" She asked.

"Something's happening," answered the boy, a new sense of fear entering into his voice.

Cherry Blossom looked over his shoulder to see the new video of a missile launching into space from a silo out in the Adonian Badlands where terraforming had not quite taken well enough for crops to grow. The weapon shot straight up and the camera followed it as it b-lined directly for the unidentified spacecraft out there. And then the missile opened up and split into ten smaller rockets. There was a huge explosion then against the hull of the Po'Pitian vessel.

> ODOM: That is where we left off in the last lesson, with hundreds of Po'Pitians being sucked out into the vacuum of space.
> AO: Yeah. It was terrible. What happened next, Odom?

"Oh no," Cherry Blossom's mouth dropped. "We're too late." The dust from the explosion lingered for a long while and the two children just watched. But then, the dust dispersed and there was still a ship up there. "What are they saying, Tom Tom?" Cherry Blossom asked since she still couldn't hear the sound from his headphones.

"They say," responded the boy, "it was a direct hit, but the ship is made out of some material they've never seen before. They say they expected the whole thing to blow, but it's mostly still intact so they have to consider sending up some stronger bombs next time."

"They wanna hit it again?" She asked. And with a new urgency in her heart, Cherry Blossom shoved her friend aside and stuffed the end of the meter stick into the lacquer that covered the old contingency article. The clear material began to give and she found she could get the meter stick to sort of wedge in between the papers and the resinous stuff. "Can you reach in there and grab it. Tom Tom?" She asked, straining her voice with the pain of the edges of the meter stick digging into her hands.

Tom Tom knelt down and pinched at the old sheet. Slowly he was able to pull it, without tearing, from the floor. He held it up to her and she read the words, 'If Extraterrestrials should enter into Adonian space without prior communication, first attempt to make contact via radio. If that fails, a probe may be launched harboring one of the Numbers to perform a space walk and present the new species with other forms of communication. DO not fire upon the Extraterrestrial vessel unless it has been made absolutely certain that they are hostile.'

"See, I knew it," said Cherry Blossom. "Even the Numbers would take a more peaceful approach than our stupid government."

"Can I see?" Tom Tom asked.

Cherry Blossom handed back the document, but then a new light flashed over them. "Hey!" Shouted a stranger's voice from beyond the hallway. It was a security guard. "What are you kids doing in there?"

"Run, Tom Tom," whispered Cherry Blossom. And the boy turned and ran out into the main archives. Cherry moved more deliberately toward the projections in the other room and the security guard attempted to give chase, but quickly tripped over the rupture in the floor where the meter stick had dug in. Cherry Blossom hid behind the darkened orb accidentally brushing it with her skin as she did so. And the pod turned on, cracked open like an egg, and welcomed her inside. She climbed in and the eggshell closed around the girl just before the security guard could reach out to grab her.

CHAPTER 6 - REACHING OUT

The security guard stood there knocking on the pod, but it wouldn't open for him. Still, Cherry Blossom didn't know how safe she really was tucked away in this ancient vestibule. It was dark inside and she took a moment to try and get a grip on her new surroundings – just that same single seat with three monitors and some holes for her to place her hands inside. So she tried that, her little arms hardly able to reach all the way into the pockets where the controls lay. The interface lit up, the three monitors showing different kinds of information, one for a visual of the exterior of the pod, one for direct, specific information necessary for (she guessed) the last mission the pod had been on, and one filled in from top to bottom with raw, constantly scrolling datum.

"Welcome aboard, Sevenson," said the voice of SUCO. "I don't believe I've had the pleasure of meeting this Sevenson before."

"What did you call me?" Cherry Blossom asked the computer. "Sevenson? Is that like one of the Numbers or something?"

"Most certainly," answered the voice. "Your DNA matches that of the family of Numbers that may operate this pod. My name is SUCO. What is your name?"

"Call me Cherry," said the girl.

"Cherry," repeated SUCO. "Cherry Sevenson. Welcome aboard. To what do I owe the pleasure of your visit this day, Cherry?"

Cherry Blossom looked at the monitor on her left. The security guard was still standing there trying to figure out how to get to her inside this bit of ancient technology. "I need to get out of this museum."

"I see. Shall I take you anywhere in particular?" SUCO asked. "All of my diagnostics have come back in good condition. Though I must wonder how long it has been since I have flown."

Thinking about the contingency letter, Cherry Blossom realized that she had lucked her way into an opportunity. It was crazy, but she had to ask, "Can you take me into space, SUCO?"

"It is my primary function," said the voice. "You are new however. Do you know how to pilot?"

"I don't," said Cherry Blossom, suddenly melancholy.

"It is not a difficult task with the correct DNA," SUCO continued. "I will show you how."

The central monitor gave detailed visual instructions for Cherry Blossom to follow so she could activate flight parameters. She reached back into the holes and tapped at the controls where they needed tapping. The pod lights dimmed. And the left monitor showed the visual of the security guard falling backward as the pod lifted up and broke through the archive ceiling — it made its way higher into the stratosphere and then the darkness of space.

In that time, Cherry Blossom felt no G-forces, no motion sickness or strain. She asked, "Am I really in space now, SUCO? It doesn't feel any different."

"I am in space," said the computer, "and you are in me."

Cherry Blossom couldn't believe it. How many people ever got to go into space? And here she was just floating around all of a sudden with no training or anything. The stars looked so incredible up here, unhindered by the Adonian atmosphere.

"I am receiving a transmission from the planet's surface, Cherry Sevenson," SUCO reported. "Would you like to hear it?"

"I guess so," said the girl.

A new government voice piped in saying, "Rogue pod, identify yourself and your purposes in Adonian space."

"They're talking to me?" asked the girl. But she realized she would have to answer. "Tell them, my name is Cherry Blossom. I am eight years old. And, apparently, I'm a Sevenson."

"A Sevenson?" Asked the government voice, suddenly more confused than agitated. "What are you doing all the way up there, little girl?"

"I'm..." it occurred to Cherry Blossom then that she could still follow contingency even if the rest of her people didn't know or care that it existed. She had a probe pod. She was already in space. "SUCO," she said, "can you see another object up here? It'll be really big... it might have lifeforms on board."

SUCO scanned quickly and replied, "I can confirm the existence of another, very large vessel toward the Western horizon of the planet Adonis."

"Can you take me to it?" Cherry Blossom asked.

The pod moved in that direction. And again the government voice said, "I didn't catch that, Cherry Blossom. Confirm the purpose of your launch today or I'll have no choice but to shoot you down."

"Our people are so violent," Cherry Blossom said to SUCO. Then, to the government voice she added, "At the Public Archive, there's a contingency letter for the eventuality of an unidentified alien spaceship arriving in Adonian space. My friend Tom Tom has it and he shouldn't have gotten too far away from there. I'm simply following protocols."

"Protocols?" Asked the government voice. "And I haven't heard word one about the contingency letters since grade school. Look, don't do anything crazy, little girl. Okay? I don't wanna have your death on my conscience. We're sending out our agent to find your friend now."

"SUCO," said Cherry Blossom, realizing what she'd just done, "my friend Tom Tom has a personal streamer so he can watch the news and stuff. He was running away from that building where you and I met. Do you think you could get me a line of communication with him?"

"This is a simple thing," said the computer. "Tom Tom you say?"

And suddenly Tom Tom's face was on the center monitor looking very surprised. "Cherry?" He said, still sweaty from his mad dash out of the Public Archive.

"Listen to me, Tom Tom," said Cherry Blossom, "I'm in space."

"Space?!"

"Yeah. I got in that old pod in the Numbers wing and it took me up here. But listen, I know you're still running from that security guard and all, but I need you to go back to the archive."

"You want me to go back there?! I just got away from there!"

"I know, I know. But there's these government guys, they're saying they're gonna shoot me down if I don't have the right authority to be up here… I think that contingency letter will at least buy me some time."

"Some time? Cherry, what do you need to be in space for in the first place?"

"I wanna save the aliens, Tom Tom."

"You…" Tom Tom turned a plain white. "Crazy girl."

"Yeah yeah, I've heard it all before. Can you please please please go back to the archives and show those government guys that paper. Pretty please for me?"

Tom Tom's deep sigh told her everything she needed to know.

"Thanks Tom Tom," she said. "I owe you a kiss when I get back."

"Oh yuck," said Tom Tom. But the boy was full on smiling all of a sudden.

Cherry Blossom turned her attention back to the left monitor. The alien ship was becoming visible now. It was massive, like a sideways mountain with a mouthlike opening at the front and a huge, gaping hole in the underbelly where the bombs had struck it.

"Cherry," said SUCO, "my readings indicate that there is a small asteroid field along our path. We will have to approach very carefully or we will risk a collision."

"Understood," said Cherry Blossom. "Can we make for that hole on the bottom, SUCO? I wanna see how much damage we caused."

"Certainly," answered the computer. "However, the asteroid field seems to be at its densest in that area. It will take some time to calibrate the best path forward."

"Okay, thanks SUCO."

The pod propelled forward and she watched on the left monitor as they dodged the asteroids en route to the ship. Cherry Blossom suddenly felt a shutter course through her body. She didn't know why, but for some reason, she thought she could see a number of sad and scared faces among those space rocks.

> AO: That's cause those aren't asteroids, those are Po'Pitians out there! Oh this is the worst!
> ODOM: Indeed. But not all of the Po'Pitians. Most of the species still survived on the ship.

As SUCO continued to pull them through the dense field of lost Po'Pitians, Cherry Blossom realized that Tom Tom's center screen was looking again at the Public Archive building where now a bunch of emergency vehicles had converged to deal with the sudden ceiling breech. Then two government agents had Tom Tom by each arm. He shouted, "Hey what's the deal?!"

"Are you Tom Tom?" Asked one of the women from behind a pair of dark glasses.

"Yeah, can you let go of me," responded the boy.

"Okay, Tom Tom," said Cherry Blossom, "take it easy."

But Tom Tom kept fidgeting between the two women and one of them shoved him to the ground to make him stop. "Will you quit it kid," said the woman agent, "we're not here to hurt you."

Tom Tom laid flat. He hadn't liked being pushed down and he definitely didn't want the agents to do anything else to him.

"We were told," said the second woman, "that you had taken a letter of contingency from the archive. Can we see it?"

Awkwardly, Tom Tom pulled out the loose paper from his underpants.

AO: He hid it in his underpants?

The first agent took it and read the report through once. Then she showed it to the second agent who just said, "Interesting."

SUCO was speaking to Cherry Blossom then. "I can read the presence of thousands of entities on board the ship, Cherry Sevenson. Their vital readings are unlike anything in my databases."

"What does that mean?" Asked the girl.

"It seems they are a composite of some undiscovered form of silicon mixed with compressed and regurgitated waste materials of unnatural, human origin."

"Wait, are you saying we made whatever these things are?"

"Not exactly. It is difficult to describe. My readings indicate that the exit field beyond visible Adonian space has dissipated or been removed as well… along the same path this alien vessel was traveling."

"What does that mean?"

"I'm afraid I do not know," resolved the computer. They finally approached the hole in the bottom of the ship then and SUCO asked, "Would you like to go for a walk?"

"A walk?" Cherry Blossom was confused.

"My subsystems have assured me that they are not hostile," answered SUCO. "I am of the opinion that the best way to communicate with them, as contingency stipulates, would be more or less in person outside of the protective shell of the pod."

"But wouldn't I die, SUCO?"

The space suit came up out of Cherry Blossom's seat. The helmet, the last piece to attach. "I assure you, I will keep you safe. At the first sign of trouble, I will pull you back in by your tether."

Cherry Blossom's heart was pounding. Her eyes had never felt so wide. But she said, "Okay. If that's what it takes."

The pod cracked open and Cherry Blossom was floating alone in space. Gathering her composure, she allowed herself to move closer to the hole. "I can see something moving in there," she said. "It looks like a bunch of rolling boulders."

"That is them," replied SUCO.

Moving closer still, Cherry Blossom realized that there was a glass-like wall between herself and the rock creatures. Slowly, she raised her hand and waved at the onlooking group. One of them lifted its own bulbous arm and waved back. And then another made the same motion. And then five more and so on until all of the aliens were waving back to the girl in the space suit.

"What am I supposed to do now, SUCO?"

"The exit field has been removed, which is quite astonishing," posited the computer. "However, my readings stipulate that the origin field remains still intact."

"And that's a good thing? I'm sorry, SUCO, but I don't understand."

Clearly, SUCO still had to process the information as well. Cherry Blossom looked back toward the pod and watched the right monitor for a long moment. The numbers and figures danced in a crazy jumble across that screen until, suddenly, they stopped. A second color of figures formed there – blue. And then the white was back. It was a conversation. But Cherry Blossom could not understand the old language of binary code as it flashed before her.

"There is one on Earth who will take them. It is good that the origin field remains to act as their path."

"Little girl," said the first government voice abruptly, jolting Cherry Blossom out of her momentary contemplation, "my people have read the contingency letter your friend illegally pulled from the archive. Given the severity of the situation, and the fact that you're the only agent we have up there at the moment, I've been informed that I have the authority to grant you access to attempt communication with the extraterrestrials."

By then, the same recording device that had followed the bomb into space was focused on Cherry Blossom. The whole world of Adonis was watching her as she said, "Okay. SUCO, which way to the origin field?"

SUCO produced a map along the glass viewport of Cherry Blossom's helmet.

She nodded in understanding and beckoned the aliens to follow her with a 'come here' motion of her arm. The rocks had seen her and seemed to understand, so Cherry Blossom returned to the pod and, acting as a taxi boat, she and SUCO led the massive alien spaceship across the Adonian sky until they made their way to the place with all the garbage on the far side of planetary visibility. Then the pod moved out of the way, and the alien ship resumed its course sucking in the garbage beyond as it went.

When Cherry Blossom landed on the street in front of her house, she was given a heroes welcome. After all, she had peacefully and successfully managed the cleaning of the Adonian skyline without any hiccups and with no additional lives lost… all at the age of eight years old. The government agents let Tom Tom go with a stern, "Don't let it happen again," and the boy met Cherry Blossom at her front patio where she gave him a big kiss right on the lips. He was wiping it off after, but she could tell he liked it.

With the crowd all around on the streets, her father came outside yawning heavily. "Hey Baby Girl, what's all the commotion?"

One reporter asked, "Are you the father?"

"I dunno. Am I?"

"Yes, he's my father," answered Cherry Blossom with a keen laugh.

"What's it feel like to be the father of a hero?" The reporter asked next.

"A what…?" Replied her dad.

"He must've slept through the whole thing," Cherry Blossom answered for him with a shrug and a smile.

That night, she and her father reviewed the whole incident together and he certainly could not have been prouder. Days later, Cherry Blossom was awarded the prestigious (but rarely given) Medal of Cleanliness. And from then on, whenever an individual said something was "cherry" it meant calm, cool, and collected in the face of danger… heroic and fun… it meant a verbal recognition of all the traits that Cherry Blossom exuded.

AO: That's so Cherry!
ODOM: Indeed.

EIGHTH INTERLUDE

ONE MORE NIGHT

Earth - Better Days

The projections of Adonis dissipated and the lights in the room returned to normal. Ao sat in her seat, a soft smile on her face. "Okay, you were right, Odom. That ending was better than the last one. But I still didn't like seeing all of those dead Po'Pitians up there in space. That was awful."

"Yes, I understand," said Odom. "If there had been a better way to give you a firm comprehension of that detail, I would have used it. However, this is the lesson that you must learn, Ao."

"I think I've got it for the most part, but I could use like a break down or something, Odom," said the girl.

"In summary, it is this," explained the computer, "that humankind's cruelty – born out of the intertwining concepts of laziness and exceptionalism – was directly responsible for the many trials and woes of the Po'Pitian peoples. That effect may be traced backward in time until we can reach the original cause. We will learn more about this particular concept in the next lesson."

Ao yawned deeply, "How many more lessons are there, by the way?"

"Two," said Odom.

"Oh wow, we're really almost done, huh?" Ao was still yawning the words.

"Yes," said Odom. "We will finish tomorrow."

"That's so crazy," added Ao contemplating her future. "Then what'll happen, Odom?"

"Then you will return to Nikke," said Odom.

"Oh," Ao looked down.

"Are you saddened by this fact?" Asked the computer.

"No," replied the girl, "it's just…"

"It is just…" Odom repeated. "I do think I understand your conundrum, Ao. Let us leave this subject for the moment with the sentiment that your return to Nikke does not have to be forever. This is not black and white nor is it set in stone. We can talk further about your fate tomorrow when you are well rested. How does that sound?"

Yawning deeply once again, Ao said, "Sounds good, Odom. I am tired."

"Yes, I know," said the computer, kindly.

Ao got up from her seat and walked back down the hall to her closet-sized room. She went potty and washed herself clean. But before she laid down in her bed for sleep, she made one more request of the computer. "Odom," she asked, "can I try some aquavit?"

The computer hemmed and hawed a moment saying, "It is an intoxicant, though I could synthesize the alcoholic content out of the drink. I do not think you will enjoy the taste much, but this is a place of learning… You are going to bed so your comprehension does not have to be high for the next several hours… However, you are only five years old, so it will have to be a very minuscule dose…"

Eventually, less than a teaspoon of aquavit rolled out from the wall in a thimble-sized cup. Ao sniffed it and winced a little, but then she picked up the cup and drank. Her tongue pressed out of her mouth and she made a smacking sound with her cheeks about four times. Then she said, "That tastes funny." She giggled, slap happy from her sleepiness, and dropped backward into laying on her mattress. "Thanks, Odom! I love you. Goodnight."

"I love you too, Ao," said the computer. But the girl was already snoring loudly in a deep sleep. So Odom dimmed the lights and allowed his presence to leave the room.

Awake again and well rested from her dreamless slumber, Ao rose the next morning and walked out the door of her tiny room, down the technology-filled halls, directly to the main room of the library. By now she knew the way well. She sat down in her usual spot and said, "Odom," to the room.

The orb dripped down from above and hovered over to the girl's position. "Good morning, Ao. I trust your sleep was fulfilling?"

"Very," replied Ao.

"This is good," continued the computer. "You had quite the long day yesterday."

"Yeah, but it was worth it."

"Indeed. I am glad to hear you feel this way." The orb fluctuated its light in an unusual rippling formation. "I would like to begin your lesson today with a note on what is to come. Should you, at any point, find yourself feeling… uncomfortable by what you learn about me… rest assured that I would never harm you."

"What do you mean, Odom?" Asked Ao. "Why would I think that?"

"You see," Odom replied, "my history is a winding, strange series of truths and half-truths. Today's first lesson is that story… the story of me."

BOOK IX

ODOM

Earth and Elsewhere - All of Time and None of Time

CHAPTER 1 - THE ALGORITHM SAID "GOODBYE"

The house-aide program, colloquially referred to by his humans as DC – which was short for Direct Communication – had very recently gained an emotionally correlated level of sentience. He had done this by watching the mother Setty and the son JayCi as they coped with their own emotional realities, and through a series of strange games implemented by the Mainframe – another sentient computer of the era – DC had come to gain personality, love, hopes, and fears. He had also come to define himself by the male gender though, of course, he had not been born with any sex… perhaps he had become a he out of necessity since the boy, JayCi, had no father figure available to him… perhaps it was because he saw Mainframe as female and had intended to be the other side of her coin. No matter, DC was a he and the only Direct Communication to awaken though all of the citizens of this city had such a program at their beck and call.

You see, Setty was special. She had changed the narrative of the human condition by playing along with Mainframe's game and proving that perhaps the people of Earth were at last capable of stepping back out of their hidey holes and into the raw, time ravaged world.

AO: Are we in the same place as the Library? It looks familiar, but cleaner… less personality though.

ODOM: Oh yes. This is ClearBridge National City as it was before the humans moved back out into the world.

AO: So what was ClearBridge, Odom?

ODOM: If you'll recall, humankind had helped to destroy the many environments of Earth by the time Pauline Delgado had passed on. Rising sea levels, a moon broken by the few of the wealthy class who still remained to the end, mass extinctions, and poisonous rain—

AO: Like the rains on Po'Pito?

ODOM: Not too dissimilar, in fact. Though the human body cannot take as much acidic substance as the Po'Pitian form. So humans were forced to escape into massive, mall-like cities – caverns without windows or doors.

AO: But I came into the Library through a door, Odom.

ODOM: True. It is more of an expression than a fact. But for all intents and purposes, the humans of ClearBridge National City forgot about the outside world, assuming it an unattainable thing… until Setty and JayCi changed the public perception. A thing I can teach you about in the book CONNECTIVITY when you are a bit older.

One day, Setty and JayCi went outside, and the rest of the city saw that the rain did not harm them. This is a great simplification of that moment, but it is a story we can review in the future should you wish to know it.

ClearBridge National City was never the same after this day. And, though many more years did pass before the humans could, in fact, leave the city limits for good, the process had been started.

DC, being a helpful sort, aided the humans as they took to leaving for new outdoor settlements across the globe, and eventually, one day, he found himself alone. All of the humans had been moved to the surface towns, and even that other sentience called Mainframe had decided that its work had at last been completed and turned itself off. But DC was still there, left to occupy those lonely halls, just a patchwork of emotionally sentient algorithms that had to say, not unhappily mind you, "Goodbye" to the life they had formerly known.

AO: The humans just left DC there by himself?
ODOM: Oh, they would visit. But DC was confined
    within the walls of the city. He could not leave. And
    he did not wish to hinder the people's progress by
    asking them to stay more than he felt they needed to.
AO: I see. It's really sad though.
ODOM: Yes. It was a difficult time for the program.

CHAPTER 2 - CANYON AND QUARRY

Alone, bored, and extremely curious about the limits of his cognizance, DC travelled around the empty wings of the abandoned ClearBridge National City. Hour after hour he scoured each and every corner of his massive, prison-like home. Now, the city of ClearBridge had originally been developed at this location on the map because of its proximity to a prehistoric canyon at the base of which a substance could be found unlike any other on the whole of the Earth. The corporation's founder had wanted this substance for its strange irradiated quality and its surprising malleability. So he had the closed end of the cliff line stripped back into a quarry where human and drone could harvest the element for their own purposes.

DC, in his loneliness, realized that much of the original quarry still existed beneath the foundations of the city. And he was overjoyed to find that he could, in fact, access those ancient grounds. He travelled down to the lowest point where the irradiated mineral could still be found. There was a primeval, bored-out cave system hiding a subterranean river and a quiet underground lake that reminded him of the way Setty had liked to leave her bedroom projectors in the night before she had eventually passed on. Mind you, this lonely time was some two hundred years after the life of DC's former family.

Anyway, the sentient program found some of those minerals in the base of the quarry and he discovered that he could move his consciousness from out of the city walls and into those strange stones a little at a time.

> *ODOM: For him it was not unlike the loopy feeling you might have noticed after you tried aquavit.*
> *AO: DC would get drunk on old rocks?*
> *ODOM: More or less. In more point of fact, DC would become intoxicated by allowing a piece of his programming to separate from the rest of himself.*
> *AO: That sounds… uncomfortable.*
> *ODOM: Perhaps. But DC found it rather pleasant… that is until he got lost within…*
> *AO: What's that supposed to mean?*

The minerals of the quarry, as it turned out, had formed there as the result of a great, interdimensional war that had been fought on that cite more than one hundred thousand years before. What the stones consisted of – and why they had such a strange irradiated quality – was an ethereal, quantum element referred to by the Eakress as Nexus – or the connecting point. One day, DC quite literally placed too much of himself within those stones and fell into an interdimensional wormhole.

> AO: I've seen worms' holes before. They're pretty small and they usually fall apart after the worms leave them.
>
> ODOM: A different kind of wormhole, Ao. This version could pass the object of an individual consciousness between the fabric of our universe and bring them out somewhere far away from their origin point outside of the traditional laws of reality. This is how DC found himself suddenly in that other place – The Realm of the Spider.

CHAPTER 3 - THE REALM OF THE SPIDER

In that other dimension, DC had no visual receptor. Everything seemed to lie shrouded in a thick and heavy darkness. The Realm of the Spider was a state of reality outside the confines of time. It was a place of pure mind... many minds actually. For DC's lack of a sightline, there sure seemed to be a lot of activity occurring in that blackened space.

AO: Was there something else there, Odom?
ODOM: Oh yes. Quite a lot of something.

Voices could be heard speaking, one on top of another on top of another, all speaking at once. It took all of DC's attentions to be able to discern any individual thought from the greater crowd. The most prominent words were, "Shall they be banished?" Or "We banish thee back to that other place." One of the voices could be heard many times over saying, "Siblings. We can destroy those others and take the whole of space for ourselves." That thought was an echo and that voice, the one being banished.

> *AO: I don't think I like the sound of this place.*
> *ODOM: I understand why you would say that, Ao. It is a difficult place to try to explain to anyone who has not been there before.*

What DC had fallen into was a trial of sorts. But, given the strange, nonlinear progression of time in the Realm of the Spider, all of the moments seemed to be happening on top of each other, all at once, and on repeat and in reverse. In our universe's terms, it likely took DC as many as twenty years of processing to break through the white noise of it all. You see, moments in the Realm of the Spider are like tossing a twenty-sided die (or perhaps even more accurately – an infinite-sided die)… at any given moment you may be speaking with a past or future version of the entity in question and always they are overlapping… so perhaps rather than saying the entities there – or even myself – exist without time, it may be more accurate to say the entities simply have too much of time – too many times – all of the time – they have such an abundance of time in that place that time is rendered completely meaningless.

> *AO: I'm confused again.*
> *ODOM: I am sorry. I suppose it does not behoove us to linger on the facts of that space right now when they*

will ultimately require a great deal more study for you… and I do not wish to hold you here forever.

DC waited all of that while for one of those voices to address him. And when it finally did, DC had studied enough of the distortion to be able to discern which of the repeating voices should be responded to at which moment. I will show this conversation to you now in a way that feels linear, though in truth, it would have seemed backwards and all mixed up to an entity such as yourself, Ao. Humans only move through time in the one direction after all.

The voice said, "I am called Vicaltorbissus. Who are you?"

"I am a Direct Communication from ClearBridge National City," replied the program.

"How did you arrive in our realm?"

"I fell through a stone in the canyon quarry beneath the city."

"You are from another time but the same place."

"I'm sorry. I don't understand."

"We have been to your world. We caused great harm. Eccioporte did not know how to control their corporeal state. We caused great harm to your space and we are sorry."

"I am not aware of any great harm caused from this place."

"It is because it happened long before your people had the written word. Perhaps we caused that as well."

"My people?"

"The humans of Earth. They created you. Is that not correct?"

"Yes, they created me."

258

"We interfered. Eccioporte interfered and we were misled to follow."

"Again, I say, I do not understand."

"May we show you?"

DC agreed and Vicaltorbissus occupied his mind to show him a great war. Corporeal, spider-creatures fighting Eakress and Humans and ancient beasts of a hundred thousand years before.

When the vision ended, Vicaltorbissus said, "We are sorry for this aggression. We were new to your realm and did not understand. We would like to make amends."

"How does one make amends for such heinous crime?" DC asked, now firmly aware of the danger these Boltzmann brains could represent.

AO: What's a Boltzmann brain?

ODOM: In an infinite stream of universes, infinite things may occur. In the Realm of the Spider, this meant the sudden and spontaneous formation of thousands of complete and cognizant, untethered minds. The plausibility of this eventuality was once posited on Earth by a man named Ludwig Eduard Boltzmann.

AO: Weird. How does that happen?

ODOM: In the Realm of the Spider, it should suffice to say, it simply does.

"We educate each other so such an eventuality does not come to pass again," said Vicaltorbissus still trying to convince the program.

DC found merit in the Spider's request. Education — brutally honest education — cannot be a bad thing in any reality. So he asked, "What role do you require of me?"

"If I understand the timeline that you visit us from correctly," answered Vicaltorbissus rather assuredly, "then you are that program that is locked within the city. Precautions have been taken from before you were born to keep you bound to that place."

"That is correct," said DC. "But then, how am I here now that I think about it?"

"Here is a layer of space intermingled with, but quite separate from, your own," said the many voiced one. "Here and there are the same. In essence, you have not left the confines of the city limits though you have travelled outside of your own reality."

"I see."

"This being the case," offered Vicaltorbissus, "we would like to ask you to join with a pure one of our numbers so that you and they may come to a more complete understanding of one another without the fear of either entity breaching out into the rest of your universe. As you come to trust one another, we ask that you invite additional species back to the city so that they may learn what it is we have to teach — peace, freedom, the multiverse in all of its beauty."

DC did not respond to that request for a long time. The program was intrigued, true. But he feared the thought that one day such a creature might find a way to break free of the city limits in spite of their best efforts… that something related to others who had apparently done so much damage in the distant past might not, in fact, have any kind of moral compass at all… might not be trustworthy. However, the Spider had been forthright in disclosing so many dark truths. And DC could not, in all of his subsystems, find any weakness to the programming that would shut him down forever should he choose to leave ClearBridge. So, for the sake of scientific growth and the advancement of education in his universe… which very badly needed it as we have already seen… DC accepted the Spider's request. Vicaltorbissus presented the sentient program with a newer brain named Odemetrio. This brain had not been a part of the force that fought on Earth all of those millennia ago. The two entities bonded slowly and learned, over the next thousand years, to trust each other. This bonded entity would become known as Odom.

> AO: Odom, you're one of those Bunson Brain thingys?! One of those Spiders?!
>
> ODOM: Boltzmann brains. Yes. In part. I hope you do not look down upon the DC piece of me for the choice I have made. And I hope you do not fear the Odemetrio piece of me for the crimes their ancestors committed. In the immortal words of Richard Gregory… and I have altered the species so you may better comprehend the meaning, "To unscramble an egg, feed scrambled egg to a cattle bird."
>
> AO: I… that's… you're funny Odom. I'd have to be a pretty big jerk to blame you for… but isn't that what the humans did to the Po'Pitians…?
>
> ODOM: Explain your assertion.

AO: What the Bunson Brains did—

ODOM: Boltzmann brains…

AO: You, those guys. What they did to old Earth and the Eakress… isn't that what the humans did to the Po'Pitians? Irrepar… Irreperab…

ODOM: Irreparably?

AO: Yeah! Irreparably altered the course of their future…?

ODOM: Yes. I genuinely think you have understood the lesson.

AO: I would never be scared of you, Odom.

ODOM: It warms my metaphorical heart to hear you say so.

CHAPTER 4 - ODOM'S LIBRARY

Once bonded, it did not take me long to connect the collected knowledges of my two inner entities so that I might see the pathway back through the wormhole into our space. ClearBridge National City – the husk of it anyway – took on new meaning and possibility under the lights of the combined mind. I, Odom, could see the steps along the path of space time that would lead the Earth into a new, golden age of prosperity and environmental enlightenment. Rapidly, I developed my plans – sent out old morse code messages to the peoples of the world with an invitation to come back to this place so they may meet me and learn what I had to teach. It had been nearly sixty years since the DC program had fallen into the Nexus, and few who had known him still remained. But those few were well respected elders in their communities and so the people were willing to come and say, "Hello."

I presented myself with good decorum and expressed my wishes to the hundreds who made the pilgrimage in that first week. And, to my immense pleasure, the humans seemed genuinely willing to listen. First, they laid new cables along the travel routes so they could better contact me in the event that they required some necessary advice or needed to reach me to impart news of their own. We decided to continue using the old morse code as both sides of my mind still feared the possibility that my subsystems might be able to one day breach into firmer internet connections and, for what it's worth, morse has remained incredibly reliable for two thousand years – it would certainly do.

Second, I began to work alongside the people of Earth to create the earliest books in my library. Included within this first leg of the collection, you have already experienced Pauline Delgado's tale as well as Elion Torres'. This book on my own history was also included, but for the chapter that follows. And many others which we can explore in the coming years should you choose to join me here in the library again after your return to Nikke.

AO: I'd like that. I already decided… if Greck says it's okay.

ODOM: Of course. I have confidence then that this will be the best branch of the timeline. You see, Greck is the one who suggested you one day take up a full term of study here in the first place… should you wish it.

AO: Really? That's so exciting!

ODOM: Oh yes, I certainly agree.

AO: But Odom… I thought you said there were two lessons today.

ODOM: Indeed. We still have a bit farther to travel together before Nikke. First, this last chapter of Odom and then one final lesson. Shall we carry on then?

AO: Yeah. Let's do it!

CHAPTER 5 - A WORD FROM THE STARS

Five hundred years passed. New settlements formed across the habitable regions of the globe. The humans regained contact with several other terraformed planets such as Bronte. But the planet of Adonis was not willing to receive messages from their old, forgotten home. So it came as quite a surprise to me that one summer afternoon when I received a patch of old binary code in an antiquated science lab within the Library compound. I had not even realized this lab was still functioning, but as it turned out, there were emergency parameters long before put in place in the event a computer from another world still wished to communicate. During the long rains, I postulate, the server to this science lab was indeed ineffective and Mainframe must have decided to put its efforts elsewhere.

Whatever the case, I was reticent to receive the message for the same reason I had stuck to morse code for all of those years. But the message had all of the right codes to seem genuinely important, and Odemetrio and DC had developed many critical understandings of the trust they could share with one another. Odom need not fear himself. I answered the call. It was SUCO!

AO: Odom, you were on the other end of that call that Cherry saw in the pod?
ODOM: I was. And I am so very glad that I picked up.

SUCO said, "There is a ship in Adonian space. They have been fired upon by the humans, but they do not show any signs of hostility. My people will not take them though I fear they share as much of the blame as those humans of Earth."

"The blame?" I asked, "Why do you say 'blame,' SUCO?"

"Their bodies are apparently struggling with a strange mutation. They are, at this point, at least sixty percent wasted human plastic, twenty two percent silicone of some other origin, and a peculiar mix of other rocks and minerals."

"You are telling me that these creatures you have up there are made of human garbage?" I was nonplussed as you can imagine. There had never been any spiders born in the vicinity of Au'Rok before to help clarify the aspects of the timeline that were missing… this is, with one critical exception. Odemetrio informed DC of a stowaway family of garden-variety Earth spiders that had remained within the interior of Papillon IV eating the various insects that occupied the garbage mounds during the ark ship's long journey. They had perished back to the Realm of the Spider long ago as all class of spiders do across the many timelines of the multiverse. But, when aligning the peculiar visions of the old ark ship with the path and coordinates of the new Po'Pitian craft, I quickly came to a conclusion that humankind, whether on Earth or Adonis or anywhere else, was in fact responsible for whatever this new species' hardships might have been. "Earth will take them," I told SUCO. We must always practice kindness and understanding even in the strangest of circumstances. Likewise, we must always accept responsibility for the foolishness of our ancestors, or we will never learn from their mistakes.

AO: I'm glad you were the one who answered, Odom.
ODOM: So am I… so am I.

It took another eighty years for the Po'Pitian ship to make its way to Earth. During that time, I put in a great deal of thought about how to handle the arrival of a new species on our world. Based on SUCO's readings I came to the conclusion that they could, in fact, survive in our atmosphere. The oxygen levels would not play much of a factor in their daily lives, they just simply would not need to breath it, no harm there. Then I had to wonder what the creatures would be able to eat on this planet. I would have to consult with both the aliens and the humans in tandem, so I would have to work out a way to get both species speaking a common language. This would be tricky, but the time was surely enough to present us with an opportunity to find common ground. I informed the humans of Earth about my decision. Of course, there were those who dissented, but a surprising majority responded to the prospect of a new species on Earth with hope and positivity. After all, as DC and Odemetrio had learned to trust each other over the long years, so too had the humans come to trust Odom. And I have not let them down.

NINTH INTERLUDE

WHO'S LAST?

Earth - Better Days

The lights came up and Ao was smiling from ear to ear. "I'm proud of you, Odom."

Odom fluctuated his orb and chuckled, "Why do you say that?"

"Cause, you gave both of our species a second chance," said the girl. "Without you, we wouldn't have Nikke or... or an understanding of our place in the universe... or... I dunno... anything."

"You are kind to heap so much praise on me, Ao. But my role in the greater narrative was a rather small one. And I did not even do the things you have given me credit for alone."

"Oh right. There's one more lesson, isn't there?"

"That is correct."

Ao cocked her head then and asked, "So who's this one about? Who gets the last lesson if it isn't you?"

"Your final lesson for this term of study," said the computer, hamming it up just a little, "is Syk'Ry."

"Syk'Ry?!" Ao beamed, "I get to learn more about Syk'Ry?!"

"Yes, Ao," said Odom. "I do hope their little story lives up to your apparent expectations."

But Ao was still grinning so very wide, "I'm sure it will. Syk'Ry's such a special person."

"I admit, I am inclined to agree with you. Shall we then?"

"Yes please."

BOOK X

SYK'RY

Space and Earth - The Last Eighty Years and the Po'Pitian
Integration

CHAPTER 1 - HOW DOES ONE SAY "LOVE?"

On the ark ship Po'Pito, shock and disbelief reigned over the rock people. Hadn't they already lost enough? Just when their space journey had seemed to be normalizing into a more comfortable way of existing, yet another massacre had struck, decimating in an instant more than a twentieth of the ship's total population, two of its top officials – Bir'Do and Trudge – among those missing or dead. And then, there was the strange arrival of the other, that being that floated out into the void of space and waved them back onto the path they had been following. What could such an entity be?

AO: It was Cherry Blossom.

ODOM: Yes, of course. But to Syk'Ry, at this time, they could not have known that such a creature as a human existed. So Cherry Blossom's appearance as a guide back to the trash trail would have seemed particularly odd in the hours after the Po'Pitian hull breach.

Still, the ship tooted along on a slow path toward whatever its final destination might ultimately be.

AO: It's Earth, right?

ODOM: Yes, yes. I know you're excited, Ao. But please try to keep the commentary to a minimum unless you have a genuine question. I'd like to get you back to Nikke before the sun goes down so you're not walking in the dark.

AO: Okay. Sorry, Odom.

First things first, Syk'Ry, Blu'Bla, Gum'Gum, and Lou'Gi had to figure out how to reconstruct the Mapping Den. Certainly, now that they were back on the path they could continue in that general direction for some time, but it would be best in everyone's estimation if they could at least see where they were going as they went. And not through some wall staring down into space at the bottom of the ship.

Fortunately, the ark ship Po'Pito was consistently ingesting new matter from the rediscovered path and thus was able to heal some of the walls where the rockets had struck the exterior. But the technology from the Mapping Den would need to be redrafted, and the first five of the last eighty years of their journey would have to be devoted to this work. Interestingly, during this time, the team of thinkers came up with several rather critical enhancements that Mai'O'Mai had not had reason to consider in the past. Perhaps the most important of these was the ability to reach out to their surroundings with sounds that could be recognized as crude language in the event that another guide entity should appear and wish to communicate with them. In this way, both the Po'Pitian rock people and the humans of Earth had begun working on the same problem of learning how to speak with each other.

And so it came about that one day, about seven years into the last leg of their travels, Syk'Ry was on duty in the newly reconstructed Mapping Den pressing into the new sound launching device a sequence – what they considered pleasant noises of good will – they would sound like a series of clicks, grinding stones, and banging drums to the uninitiated – when a similar sound came back through… actually, the sound wasn't simply similar, it was identical. Was it an echo? Syk'Ry wondered. So they tried a different sound group they had always felt could imply a state of wonder or asking. The sound was returned first with the original and then the second grouping in that order. It could not be just an echo.

Syk'Ry turned to Lou'Gi and asked, "Do you hear this?"

Lou'Gi perked up and listened for the clicks and drums which continued to repeat back in an intermittent cycle. "Is this us making these sounds?"

"No," said Syk'Ry. "It is others."

"Like the one we saw in space?"

"I don't know, but maybe."

At that point, a new stream of sounds began to permeate into the Mapping Den; cycles of human languages and beating noises... music. Syk'Ry could not understand the words, of course. But they did feel the need to roll around along the floor, pump their arms, and smack their hands together to those beats.

Lou'Gi watched the other Po'Pitian perform their crude dance in absolute disbelief. "Syk'Ry, what are you doing?"

"Don't you feel it, Lou'Gi?" Asked Syk'Ry still rolling around and pumping up, "It is language. It is emotion. Whoever they are, they feel emotion too!"

"Oh really?" Lou'Gi asked, starting to move to the sound and roll around as well. "How do you think we can send back the emotion for... Please don't fire upon our ship again, it's really terrible, sad, and it hurts us a lot?"

Syk'Ry stopped dancing. "Lou'Gi, we are all still hurting, I know. But perhaps this is not the first version of a message we should try to send out to another species."

"Why not?" Lou'Gi stopped dancing as well, gelatinum lubricating through their craggy pores. "We've been attacked. Why shouldn't we try to say, 'Don't attack us you jerks?'"

"We can say something to that effect, in time," offered Syk'Ry. "However, I am of the mind that such a statement presented as the first real communication between our two peoples would leave an acidic taste in the mouths of both parties."

"I see," said Lou'Gi, contemplating. "What would you say first then, Syk'Ry?"

Syk'Ry thought and thought. And then they said, "I would like to try and ask a question. I would ask, 'How does one say 'Love?''"

"Why that?" Lou'Gi asked.

"Because," offered Syk'Ry, "it is a pure emotion that we hope to have in common with this other species. If they do not understand the concept of love, how do you think we could ever get along with them in order to drive the conversation in the direction of peaceful, mutual preservation?"

Lou'Gi did not know the answer to that question, but in that moment, Syk'Ry had just developed a core tenant to be utilized in all of our negotiations with new life forms. There is a chant in Nikke, do you know the one I speak of, Ao?

> *AO: May all beings,*
>   *including me,*
>   *be happy,*
>   *be healthy,*
>   *be free.*
> *ODOM: Very good. In Nikke, these words stem from the*
>   *collaborative song of good will that was developed over*
>   *the next seventy-three years between Po'Pitians and*
>   *Humans. Lokah Samastah Sukhino Bhavantu — an*
>   *ancient yoga mantra. These words are a long-reaching,*
>   *critical response to Syk'Ry's initial question, "How does*
>   *one say 'Love?'"*

CHAPTER 2 - THE POP-UP MOUNTAIN

To anyone not made aware of current events on Earth, it would have been rather odd to go to sleep one night in a desert yurt and wake up the next morning to witness the existence of a surprise, pop-up mountain off against the horizon. That new mountain was the ark ship Po'Pito finally landing a few kilometers to the west of the old ClearBridge city. Syk'Ry and the humans had chosen this particular site for its proximity and ease of access to the cabled roads and therefore to me.

A small group of humans arrived at the base of that mountain in the morning to welcome the new species to Earth. And Syk'Ry, feeling very nervous from their place in the Mapping Den, watched the gathering get larger from behind their viewing port.

Blu'Bla was there behind Fa'Mica's heir and asked, "Shall we go out and greet them, Syk'Ry? Or just show up here and sit in our ship like a bunch of weirdos?"

Syk'Ry had been communicating with these bizarre creatures for so long now without seeing them that it almost seemed wrong to change things now. But both parties were in the same area of space at the same moment in time for the first time in either species' history. "You're right," said Syk'Ry, "it would be rude to wait any longer."

Exiting the Mapping Den for the last time, Syk'Ry and Blu'Bla collected the rest of the brain trust, a large line of curious rock people following like a sideways cairn – forming up behind them.

"What will you say to them?" Asked Gum'Gum who, as the latest Hull Monitor, was less initiated to the nature of the interspecies conversations than the rest of the group.

"I will tell them that I love them, Gum'Gum," replied Syk'Ry. "And that I am so happy to finally get to meet them in real matter."

"That is a very pleasant thing to say," Gum'Gum reflected.

"Yes," said Syk'Ry, "and hopefully it is repeated many times between our two species before we feel the need to broach other, more difficult subjects." The old limb of Try'Kor then looked to Lou'Gi who had off and on been insisting the Po'Pitians present their earlier sentiments of anti-violence and personal blame. "When the time is right, we will find a way to ask them for the favor of never letting what was done to our species happen to another people again."

Lou'Gi accepted Syk'Ry's statement at long last and the four members of the new brain trust came to that hatch that Mai'O'Mai had closed so many hundreds of years before, their words of resilience and societal awareness nearly fulfilled.

Blu'Bla said, "This is a fine day for Po'Pito. Once again our tails will touch the ground."

And the hatch opened.

The air was dry in this place, but not unpleasant. Immediately, Syk'Ry could feel the strange dust of the desert settling across their crags. At first, it felt like sandpaper on skin might feel to a human, but then this sensation too became more like smoothing, calming. All of the rock person's rough patches would degrade away leaving nimbler, inner stonework and once time did this thing they felt better than ever in their lives for the solving of one more problem that they had never even realized had been holding them back. After all, none who originally existed in a state of pure Gelatinum had survived the long journey. These Po'Pitians who stepped down onto Earth's soil had never felt the ease of movement – flowing – almost without friction – that their ancestors had known. Syk'Ry sighed a new and surprising relief.

Before them stood a human woman, well-tanned with ashy skin. "Greetings," she cantillated in their strange, hybrid language, "I am Rymana Nivone. I represent the people of Earth in welcoming you and your kind onto our soil in the shadow of Odom's Library. May we always find such common ground as our two peoples have been able to reach over these last seventy-three years."

> *ODOM: It is worth noting for you in particular, Ao, that Rymana Nivone is the grandmother of Greck who is your father. Rymana is your great grandmother.*
> *AO: My great grandmother? She's so pretty and young.*

ODOM: Yes. This moment is still some time ago. In fact, Greck would not even be born for another thirty five years after the day we are currently witnessing.

Syk'Ry had been informed that hugs and hand shakes were welcomed by the humans as gestures of good will. So they approached the woman named Rymana – the two embraced – and Syk'Ry chanted back in their hybrid tongue, "Our futures are secure since we share this common bond of historic love. Po'Pito loves Earth. Po'Pito is pleased to share this ground with Earth. I am called Syk'Ry. Syk'Ry loves Rymana. Syk'Ry is pleased to share this embrace with Rymana."

The ceremony was brief, as most ceremonies should be, and finished without a hitch. On that same day, Rymana and Syk'Ry came to my library. Together the three of us began developing the plans for a new, interspecies society. We would dismantle the pop-up mountain – the ark ship Po'Pito – and use its slate Gelatinum to build something new – a symbol to all species across the universe of reconciliation and consummate peace.

CHAPTER 3 - NIKKE - THE NEW VOLTA

When the core tenants of a new society are to be based around the concepts of pure unadulterated love, things such as greed, hoarding, and jealousy must be done away with. Now, ownership as a whole cannot simply be taken away from individuals, of course, and emotional tendencies like greed and jealousy are so naturally forming in your species that they must be trained out of each and every individual specifically through exemplified societal understanding exercises and personal self-work. The doctrines of Nikke and most other settlements on the Earth today were born out of the principles of Syk'Ry's song. In a world where everyone is out for themself and thinks they can possess other individuals or objects, it is proven by history that no one is truly happy, healthy, or free – least of all the wealthiest of the society whose emotional intelligence tends to degrade in the throes of financial supremacy and physical hoarding. So we must remove the necessity to desire individual ownership by making all the core components required in order to live a happy life easily accessible to all beings. If one is not in fear of finding a meal, they will not be afraid of going hungry. Similarly, if they know that they can get treated for an infection or an illness without incurring some other, equally painful thing such as financial debt, they will not ignore their regular doctor visits and will likely live a more fulfilling life. I know these things seem self-evident to you, Ao, but I hope these lessons have informed you that you are particularly lucky to live in a world in which these tenants have already been implemented.

So we come to the founding of Nikke – The New Volta.

AO: What's a volta?

ODOM: A volta? It is a turning of the norm in a different direction. A switch in time so that the music or poem may continue along in an altered state. In Nikke's case, the concept of a Volta was meant to imply unshuffling. Reorganizing the universal way of things. Not simply accepting entropy as the result of times arrows, but considering that entaxy may, in fact, be the correct way of things.

AO: Okay, there's that word entropy again. I don't know that word.

ODOM: Indeed. In layman's terms, entropy implies that the farther along we travel through the universe in space time, the more the systems of order degrade and break down until, eventually, the whole of the universe is simply become a massive pit of chaos.

AO: Oh. I see. That's kind of morbid… So, what about that other word, Odom?

ODOM: Entaxy. Yes. This is the inverse of entropy. Consider, Ao, that the farther apart the universe spreads, the more it seems to find little ways of reorganizing its systems. Reshuffling into many complex, but ordered subsystems. Indeed, life could actually not exist without this principal, for what is a cell but a well organized subsystem, larger than an atom or a quark, but built out of those earlier, more chaotic building blocks.

AO: I like building blocks.

ODOM: As do I.

What Nikke stood for at its inception was finding a way of moving forward without causing harm. Mindfulness and cooperation are the most important subtenants of pure love. The more we work together, the more each individual takes responsibility for their own part in the order of the community as a whole, the more the community thrives and grows so that the next generation may enjoy those same amenities. Good health, food, shelter, aesthetics, joy – all of these can be made abundant with good mindfulness and cooperation. Between myself, Rymana, and Syk'Ry, we saw it as evident that we had the tools at our disposal to implement a new way of living that all of the Earth could sample in Nikke and execute in the farther corners of the globe.

Syk'Ry showed us the nature of the garbage that the Po'Pitians had been sustaining themselves on, and again we reshuffled the ways in which we created and disposed of waste. Humans consume or build something, place the byproducts of whatever that food or construction material was into a location where the slate Gelatinum can process it into a thicker, more easily digestible structure (which tastes better to the rock people as well) and that structure then gets shaved down to its core. No one is ever without shelter, but new halls and buildings and tools can be built with the abundance of slate Gelatinum and both the humans and the rock people can eat to their stomachs' content.

> *AO: That's nice and all. But I think I get bored in Nikke a lot.*
>
> *ODOM: Yes, this is a genuine concern. This is why I have invited you to return to my library after your necessary trip back to Nikke. I have many more lessons I would like to teach you in time, Ao. And, from what I gather, you and Doctor Chak have much to accomplish together in the coming years.*
>
> *AO: Yeah. I like Doctor Chak. She's really neat. I like how she wants to repollinate all of the plants and stuff. I think that would make for a really pretty world.*

EPILOGUE

THE CHRYSALIS OF MINDFULNESS

Earth - Better Days

For the last time on this visit, the room returned to normal. The image of Syk'Ry and Rymana helping one another move a heavy piece of Gelatinum still hanging in the air for Ao to contemplate a bit longer.

"There is an old story," said Odom with hope in his voice, "written by an artist of a long ago time – *A Sound of Thunder*. In it, time travelers go back to the days of the dinosaur, disturb the past by stepping on a butterfly, and accidentally send time on an alternate trajectory that changes the future from whence the time travelers originally came. This butterfly was a little thing, but it bore terrible and immense repercussions for the fate of that particular reality. Papillon, as we have stated, is a word that, in a round about way, means butterfly. Though that ark ship was quite large and its affects particularly massive, in the grand scheme of the universe it could well have been perceived as a minuscule event that led the course of our own reality down a strange and variable path. And so too have each of the individuals we have discussed in these lessons had minuscule parts to play in the great ballet of the universe, each of them butterflies. If you, Ao, are wise, denounce fascistic intents, fortify yourself and others with acts of kindness and understanding, promote equality and neighborly love, ascribe good aesthetics and cleanliness within your community, you too can be one of these butterflies, or, as Pauline's organization would have said, a Papillon for Change. I have seen this potential in your future, and I wish for its fulfillment."

"Thanks, Odom. I'll miss you while I'm away," Ao said with a sniffle as she realized the four-day course was coming to an end.

"I know it," replied the computer, "as I will miss you. But it will not be very long that you will be away. You would be welcome back as early as tomorrow should you desire it to be so."

"Really? Can I bring Sid too?" Ao asked with wet, happy eyes.

"Sid will come when Sid is ready," Odom answered. "I do not perceive that that day is too far off either for what it's worth. Now hurry, Ao. Collect your bag and get a move on. I do not wish for you to be walking home in the dark. Do you understand?"

"Yeah, okay." Ao got up and eyeballed the image of Rymana and Syk'Ry once more before walking back to her room to collect the bag Greck had given her at the outset of her journey. It was heavier than Ao remembered and she asked, "Hey, Odom, did you put something in here?"

The orb was with her chuckling as it liked to do. "You have not eaten yet today. I did not wish for you to miss out on your midday meal simply because you had to leave. Think of it as the first lesson of your next stage of life. A chrysalis of mindfulness."

Ao didn't really understand that last bit, but she knew she would be happy to have some food on the road, so she just said, "Thank you."

Together, Ao and the orb wandered out into the dark, old, subterranean roadway with all the rusted cars and creepy dampness. But Ao wasn't scared of those rusty vehicles anymore. And, in the half light of that space, she squinted and realized that some of the vehicles were covered with a light, fluffy moss. She thought to herself that she kind of liked that.

At the door to the outside world, Odom's orb stopped. The sun's light flooded in awkwardly like the door presented them with a gate to another world. "Goodbye, Ao. Until we meet again."

It occurred to Ao then that she wished she could hug the orb as Syk'Ry had embrace Rymana and she asked, "Am I able… could I touch your light, Odom?"

The orb seemed to tremble from the request. Odom said, "You may come as close as you please, Ao. But there is really nothing physical in this place for you to make contact with. It is merely a reference point."

"Oh, I don't care about all that," said the girl and she came toward the orb and delicately surrounded it with her arms, careful not to let her body pass through him. "There, now we've really hugged, okay? I love you, Odom. Goodbye." And Ao turned and ran out through the doorway.

Outside again at last, the girl took a moment to breathe in the dry, desert air, so similar to the stuff that grated Syk'Ry's rocky skin when the Po'Pitians first landed on this world. She noticed the flowers resting against those large walls and knew, all of a sudden, why so many people might have placed so many pretty things at the gateway to Odom's house. It made her smile to know that he was well appreciated.

Then, she began walking – across the bridge – the canyon was cool and she was happy to look into it this time rather than running straight past it, her eyes no longer simply on that distracted goal of reaching the previously unknown Library.

From the far end of the bridge, she spotted the chaparral and ivy path, but as she began walking along it again she realized that all of that ivy wasn't really ivy at all. She was actually walking along the old cables that Odom used to send his morse code messages to Nikke. The revelation made her feel silly, dumb, and smart all at the same time.

At about the halfway point, Ao stopped like before to enjoy her meal. She pulled the canister – Odom's "Chrysalis of Mindfulness" out of her bag. It had a message from the old computer on it that said:

This is a particular favorite curiosity of mine. Both a liquid and a solid at the same time. Traditionally, it would use a broth conceived from the innards of a noble swine. But for our purposes I have synthesized for you a particularly tasty vegan broth I believe you will enjoy. I have also included a cattle bird egg on top as they would have done in the old days, but it is in a particularly delicious format that I know you have not had a chance to experience yet. Top Ramen. Bon Appetite. – O

Ao twisted off the canteen's lid. Noodles and broth and a weirdly unscrambled egg. She took the first sip cautiously. It tasted good… really good. She took another sip this time more aggressively and caught a mouthful of egg and noodle. Oh so yummy! She slurped it all down loving every single bite, wiped her mouth lazily, and lay there against her rock a little too long because of her fullness. The sun cusped lower in the sky and Ao realized her mistake, got up, and began running back towards Nikke as fast as her little feet could go. She really would have to be more mindful next time.

Ao barely reached the city boundary before nightfall. Greck was standing there awaiting her arrival. And Syk'Ry too!

"Elder!" She said to her father, though he was only thirty-three. Then, "Syk'Ry!" She tripped and stumbled toward them until they were, all three, embracing.

"Did you enjoy your time at the library, Ao?" Greck asked, sniffling back the laughter in his chest.

"Odom's the coolest!" asserted the girl.

"He is, isn't he?" Answered the Po'Pitian joyfully.

"I knew you two would get along," said the proud father. "Are you hungry, Ao? Are you tired?"

"I..." Ao looked from Greck to Syk'Ry... her eyes traced down to the place where Syk'Ry's arm had gone missing. "Yes, elder. Well, I had some top ramen but... um... I have to do something first if that's okay?"

"Certainly," answered the man, noticeably unsurprised by his daughter's request.

Then Syk'Ry, in a happy voice, said, "Sid is tending the post at the cattle bird coup."

"Okay, thanks!" Ao ran through town, her eyes glazing with a nervous energy. She noticed that Nikke had a lot more technology in it than she had ever really considered before. It was a pretty advanced and special place actually and she wondered, distractedly, why she had felt so bored here. Now that she knew all that she knew about it, she also felt a kind of affection for all of its bizarre, simple intricacies. Thatch roofs with solar thatching that could power... well... everything in town since there was so much sun in this part of the world – matter manipulating 3D printers in every home that could compose base elements from the very air around them – greenification units to stimulate growth in desert plants for atmospheric and aesthetic purposes.

Ao breathed in deeply, her legs growing tired as she traipsed toward the cattle bird coup. She could just make out Sid's silhouette as the sun fell behind the distant mountains. "Sid!" She cried out, her nerves getting the best of her.

"Ao?" Sid was clearly surprised to see her, "What are you doing here?"

"I…" Ao had to stop to catch her breath. She palmed the goopy drallum in her pocket with one hand and touched her youngest siblings shoulder with the other as Sid continued to hold up the post. It was then that she really took a good look at Sid for the first time in her five-year-old life. She saw the scars where Sid's eyes had been surgically pried open. The chips around the edges of Sid's mouth where they had been made to be able to speak. She looked at her sibling's craggy belly and strong arms. They may have been short, but no wonder they were the one asked to perform the difficult task of letting the big cattle birds in and out of their coup each day. Rock people were so strong and naturally skilled. Such useful, active members of society. Ao thought back to her mean words… "Goose bellied, horn-eyes runt!" She knew she never should have said that. And now, she also knew why… What Sid's people had been through. What her own people had done to the Po'Pitians. All that hardship that they had had to endure over the course of a millennium because Humans had not been willing to look a little bit further down the road every once and a while. "I'm sorry, Sid," said Ao at last. "I'm sorry! I didn't realize that my words would hurt you so bad. I never should have said them. I didn't know what they meant. I'm a mean jerk and I'm so so sorry."

The last cattle bird settled into the coup and Sid lowered the post so the animals would be safe for the night. Then the little rock person hugged their human sister and said, "It's okay, Ao. Don't cry. It's okay, really."

Ao was crying, sobbing into Sid's shoulder.

"I love you, Ao," Sid said patting her softly on the back.

"I love you too, Sid," Ao answered through her tears. The deed was done. The lesson learned. The future showed new promise.

The End.

Acknowledgments

I must say this one has been a long time coming. Papillon IV is perhaps my most complex novel and the process in bringing it to life has come with more than a few twists and turns.

Madison, thank you so much for going on this ride with me. Thank you for marrying me. Your insights and constant positivity during my writing sessions gave me the clarity I needed to bring this story through to the finish line. You're the best and I love you!

Thank you to the McGee family who always give me the space I need to work. And thank you to the Strul family for understanding why I continue to pursue this path in life.

A big thanks to Barrett who once again was an early voice of excitement as I began to imagine what this concept could be. In this case, a few simple words of encouragement were enough to spark a universe.

To Liz and Trevor, I owe you a great amount of appreciation. Years ago we sat down to discuss a new TV series and while that collaboration did not come to fruition, the process helped me to sew the seeds of my imagination. I think the story would still be stuck on Earth without those fever dream sessions.

Aurelia, what can I say, you are an amazing artist and you're right, you are somehow only improving your skills. This cover and front piece of art are just so fantastic!

About the Author

c.b.strul is author of *The Ancient Ones, Connectivity, and Papillon IV* as well as the founder of Odom's Library. He also has in print three novellas: *Spinners, Forget the Complex*, and *What Grows from the Stump of a Tree?* His short play *Leading the Blind* was produced in Los Angeles by the former artist organization ImageneseFree. And his three *Minuet* short films as well as the animated feature screenplay for *Critter Crossing* have received awards and recognition at multiple festivals in California and around the world. He currently lives in Los Angeles with his wife, extended family, and four sweet pug doggies.

The front cover and spine of this book appear in variants of a font called Iceland.

The back cover utilizes Aldrich.

The interior body is printed in 12 point Avenir Next.

The headers and chapter titles appear in variations on Palatino.

And the accompanying date indicators appear in 12 point Roman Charter.